"Emotionally charged . . . will not easily be forgotten."
—*Romantic Times* (4 ½ stars, Gold Medal, Top Pick)

LET THE CHURCH SAY AMEN

#1 *Essence* magazine bestseller

One of *Library Journal*'s Best Christian Books for 2004

"Billingsley infuses her text with just the right dose of humor to balance the novel's serious events."
—*Library Journal* (starred review)

"Amen to *Let the Church Say Amen*. . . . [A] well-written novel."
—*Indianapolis Recorder*

"Emotionally compelling. . . . Full of palpable joy, grief, and soulful characters."
—*The Jacksonville Free Press* (FL)

"Her community of very human saints will win readers over with their humor and verve."
—*Booklist*

MY BROTHER'S KEEPER

Her award-winning debut novel

"This is a keeper."
—*The Daily Oklahoman*

"Poignant, captivating, emotional, and intriguing. . . . A humorous and heart-wrenching look at how deep childhood issues can run."
—*The Mississippi Link*

Also by ReShonda Tate Billingsley

My Brother's Keeper

Let the Church Say Amen

Help! I've Turned Into My Mother

I Know I've Been Changed

Have a Little Faith
(with Jacquelin Thomas, J. D. Mason,
and Sandra Kitt)

Everybody Say Amen

Can I Get a Witness?

The Devil Is a Lie

Holy Rollers

A Good Man Is Hard to Find

And check out ReShonda's Young Adult titles:

Nothing But Drama

Blessings in Disguise

With Friends Like These

Getting Even

Fair-Weather Friends

Friends 'Til the End

Caught Up in the Drama

Drama Queens

The Pastor's Wife

ReShonda Tate Billingsley

POCKET BOOKS

New York London Toronto Sydney

Pocket Books
A Division of Simon & Schuster, Inc.
1230 Avenue of the Americas
New York, NY 10020

This book is a work of fiction. Names, characters, places, and incidents either are products of the author's imagination or are used fictitiously. Any resemblance to actual events or locales or persons, living or dead, is entirely coincidental.

Copyright © 2007 by ReShonda Tate Billingsley

First Pocket Books paperback edition May 2011

POCKET and colophon are registered trademarks of Simon & Schuster, Inc.

For information about special discounts for bulk purchases, please contact Simon & Schuster Special Sales at 1-866-506-1949 or business@simonandschuster.com.

The Simon & Schuster Speakers Bureau can bring authors to your live event. For more information or to book an event contact the Simon & Schuster Speakers Bureau at 1-866-248-3049 or visit our website at www.simonspeakers.com.

Cover design by Kristine V. Mills, cover photo of woman by George Kerrigan, church by Getty Images

Manufactured in the United States of America

10 9 8 7 6 5 4 3 2 1

ISBN 978-1-4516-1163-2
ISBN 978-1-4165-5445-5 (ebook)

For Myles Julian Joseph

acknowledgments

Here I am, on book number ten, and at the part of writing I've been dreading—the acknowledgments. These dang things have caused more drama than the actual stories in my books. (My cousin just started back-speaking to me after I left her name out of the previous books and nobody at her church believed we're related.) Oh, and don't let me forget _____ (insert name here—you know who you are), who raked me over the coals for days because so-and-so's name came before hers/his.

So having said that, here are my acknowledgments this go-round . . .

Thank you, God.

Thank you, everybody else.

There, that ought to cover everyone.

Until the next book, enjoy.

ReShonda

prologue

1993

Terrance couldn't get inside fast enough. He rammed his key in the lock, opened the door, and raced in the house. After slamming the front door closed, he leaned against it and tried to catch his breath.

It was the first time he'd been able to think straight in the last fifteen minutes.

"Boy, what have you gotten yourself into now?"

Terrance looked up to see his great-aunt Eva towering over him, the usual disappointed look across her face. Her head was adorned with pink hair rollers, and her canary yellow bathrobe was tightly tied with a blue sash. "And don't even fix your lips to lie to me." She wagged her finger in his face. "You sweating like a runaway slave, all out of breath." She stepped closer, narrowed her eyes at him, then wiggled her nose. "Terrance Deshaun Ellis, have you been drinking?"

Terrance immediately tried to get his story together. "Naw, Auntie. Why you trippin'?"

Eva scooted her large frame closer to him and sniffed. "You *have* been drinking." She swung her left arm and hit him on the side of the head. "You smell like a moonshine factory!"

Terrance ducked out of the way before his aunt could deliver another blow. "Go on with that, Aunt Eva!"

"I swear to God, you gonna drive your grandma to an early grave!" Eva barked. "It's Christmas Eve and you got her worried to death because your little narrow behind is out running the streets doing God only knows what. Thinking you grown."

"I'm almost grown," Terrance mumbled, rubbing his temple. His head was pounding, his vision was blurred, and he was still sweating bullets over what had just happened.

"Fifteen is far from grown!" Eva took a deep breath, trying to calm herself down. She shook her head as sadness began to frame her pear-shaped face. "Terrance, when are you going to stop causing so much trouble?"

Terrance closed his eyes and groaned. He was not in the mood for a lecture—again. His three great-aunts lectured him nonstop, chastising him for "breaking his grandmother's heart."

"We done got you out of jail twice, been up to your school more times than we can count cuz you always fighting. I pray round the clock, and you still won't do right." Eva sighed. "You won't go to church. You won't listen. I just don't know what to do about you. My sister is out there right now, roaming the streets at three in the morning looking for your tail. I told her, we just need to turn you loose, because the devil has a hold on you."

Terrance desperately wanted to ask his aunt if they could finish this conversation another time. It's not like he didn't know it by heart anyway. His grandmother and her three sisters had raised him since his mother died when he was just two years old. And he'd been more than a handful for them.

He definitely didn't feel like hearing a lecture right now because his mind kept replaying the past fifteen minutes. *How had he ended up behind the wheel of a stolen car?* Everything was a big blur. He remembered hanging out with his boys. He remembered the drinks—all of the drinks. Then, the next thing he recalled was the sirens and his ditching the car two streets over and running for his life.

Luckily, Terrance didn't have to listen to much more because the doorbell rang, and he decided to use that as an opportunity to escape upstairs to his room.

"I'm not through with you, boy!" Eva called out when she noticed him dart toward the stairs. "This is probably your grandmother, poor thing. Probably locked herself out. I know she's tired . . ."

Terrance let her voice trail off as he made his way upstairs. He had just taken off his shirt and was getting ready to plop down across his bed when he heard his aunt scream, "Nooooo!"

He immediately raced back down the stairs. Eva was leaning against the doorframe; two sheriff's deputies were trying to hold her up. Terrance froze. They'd come for him. They'd figured out what had happened and had come to take him to jail. This would be his third arrest and he was sure to do some real jail time.

Terrance was just about to make a run for it when he saw Eva drop to her knees and scream, "She can't be dead, she just can't. No, Lord, no!"

Terrance suddenly forgot all about his own troubles. "Wh . . . who's dead?" he asked as he slowly walked toward his aunt. He had a sickening feeling in the pit of his stomach. Eva looked up at him, tears blanketing her face. That in itself told Terrance something was seriously wrong because Aunt Eva was a hard-nosed woman who didn't even shed a tear when her husband of twenty years walked out on her.

"Who's dead?" Terrance repeated.

Eva pulled herself up off the floor. "Oh, Terrance." She held out her arms as she walked toward him. "It's Essie. Your grandmother was in a horrible car accident. They said she's dead!" Eva pulled Terrance into her chest and sobbed.

Terrance's body began to shake as Eva's words set in. He broke free from his aunt. "No, no, no." Terrance continued to shake his head in denial as Eva struggled to pull herself together.

"Ma'am, is there anyone we can call for you?" the sheriff's deputy asked.

"My sisters. I've got to call Mamie and Dorothy Mae," Eva muttered as she walked around the living room in a daze, looking for the phone.

"Why you comin' up in here with this?" Terrance said to the deputies, his voice shaky. "My grandma ain't dead. She's just out looking for me. She'll be right back."

"I'm sorry, sir," the other deputy said. "She hit a tree. She was killed on impact."

The look on the deputy's face told Terrance this wasn't some cruel joke. Suddenly, every bad thing he'd recently done flashed through his mind, including the last fifteen minutes. "Oh, my God. This is all my fault!" Terrance dropped to his knees and buried his head in his hands. Tears began to fall as he recalled his grandmother's last words to him that afternoon.

"Son, I'm praying that the Lord will change your troubled ways," she'd said when she caught him going through her purse. "I love you and I'm never gonna give up on you."

Terrance had blown her off, silently cursing that she'd caught him before he could get some money. What he wouldn't do now to turn back time.

chapter 1

"Boy, you sho' can preach!" Chester Edwards let out a hearty laugh as he slammed his oversize palm on Terrance's back.

Even though he stood a good four inches taller than Chester's small, five-feet-eight frame, Terrance had to catch himself from falling over. He forced a smile and nodded at Chester. "Thank you, Brother Edwards. I try my best."

"Hmph, try? My handsome nephew just got a natural talent," Eva said as she brushed a piece of lint off Terrance's robe. She smiled, admiring his strong features, his smooth, coffee brown skin and cheekbones that could cut glass.

Mamie walked to the other side of Terrance and draped her arm through his. "And what else would you expect, Chester, when he was raised by four of the most wonderful women in the world?"

Terrance blushed. His aunts were so proud of him

now. After his grandmother's death, they had stepped up their mothering roles. He'd worked hard to turn his life around. He had stood at his grandmother's funeral and promised God that he would make his grandmother proud.

Terrance dumped his friends, buckled down in school, and shocked everyone when on the one-year anniversary of Essie's death he said he wanted to give his life to God. He went on to college at Clark Atlanta University, then seminary school at Arkansas Baptist College. Not too long after moving back to Houston, he became pastor of Lily Grove Missionary Baptist Church.

Terrance couldn't help the warm feeling that filled his heart when he thought of how happy his grandmother would be to see him as a preacher, of all things, especially at Lily Grove, the church he'd grown up in.

Chester let out a grunt, bringing Terrance out of his thoughts. "It's a wonder that boy know how to do anything the way y'all old hens are fawning over him all the time like he's the Second Coming." Chester quickly looked at Terrance. "No disrespect, Pastor."

"None taken, Brother Edwards." Terrance chuckled. Both men stopped talking as a tall, older woman in a short, tiger-print miniskirt and satin-fringed shawl sauntered out of the sanctuary.

"Afternoon, Pastor," she said, trying to sound sexy. "That was a wonderful sermon you preached today."

"Thank you, Sister Florence." Terrance turned to the beautiful, young woman standing behind her. "Sister Savannah, did you enjoy the service today?"

Savannah nodded. "I did."

"Then why did you sleep through half of it?" Florence cackled as she tossed the strands from her honey blond wig out of her face.

Savannah looked uncomfortable, but quickly replied, "Grandma, you know I was not asleep."

"I don't know nothing but what I saw, and I saw your eyes closed."

Terrance smiled. "I'm sure Sister Savannah was just deep in prayer."

Savannah returned his smile. "That's exactly what I was doing, Pastor." Her eyes lit up as she looked him up and down.

Florence looked at her granddaughter strangely. "Girl, are you openly flirtin' with the pastor?" She laughed. "Please. Tell her, Reverend. As if she stood a snowball's chance of being with a man like you." Florence continued laughing, ignoring the hurt look across Savannah's face. "Come on here, gal. I done told you 'bout them pipe dreams. Like Reverend Ellis would even be caught dead with somebody like you," she mumbled as she made her way down the steps.

Savannah couldn't mask the hurt as she looked at Terrance. She seemed like she wanted to say something, but just clutched her purse tighter and took off after her grandmother.

"That's a doggone shame the way that woman does that child," Chester said as he watched them walk down the sidewalk.

"I guess we just invisible? She didn't even acknowledge us and we're standing right next to you," Eva snapped to Terrance. She turned up her nose. "And look at her." Florence had stopped and was wiggling to pull down her skirt, which had risen up her thighs. "What is that woman, sixty-five? And still trying to dress like she's twenty-one?"

Mamie echoed her sister's disgust. "She's looking like a broke-down Eartha Kitt. And got the nerve to think she's still sexy. Hussy. I don't know why she even bother coming to church. Like she even knows God."

"How do you know what's in her heart?" Terrance admonished.

"Whatever," Mamie said, blowing his question off. "What self-respecting, decent Christian woman, especially someone her age, comes to church in a tiger-print miniskirt?"

"I don't know," Chester replied, licking his lips as he watched Florence walk down the street. "I think she is nice-looking, and that body, Lord, have mercy."

"Don't you have to get home and feed your chickens, Chester?" Dorothy Mae snapped, her face suddenly becoming flush with anger.

"Pigeons. I got pigeons!" he snapped back.

"They're all the same," Dorothy Mae nonchalantly replied.

"They is not! You ever heard of Kentucky Fried Pigeon?" Chester stomped down the steps of Lily Grove. Dorothy Mae had hit a sore spot.

"And if you ever need to communicate with somebody and yo' telephone don't work, don't come asking to use my pigeons!" he called out as he stomped off.

"I promise you ain't got to ever worry about that!" Dorothy Mae yelled after him.

"Now, Dorothy Mae, why you agitating Chester like that?" Eva said, a smile forming across her wrinkle-free face. Eva was almost seventy, but could easily pass for fifty. Years of a careful regime of Dove soap and water had proved to be good to her.

"Cuz ever since he dumped her, she got to give him a hard time," Mamie cackled, her hefty frame jiggling as she teased her petite sister.

"He didn't dump me," Dorothy Mae protested. "It was the other way around and you know it. After Ernest died, God rest his soul, I couldn't keep Chester from sniffing around me. He wanted me, not the other way around."

"Excuse me, ladies, but as much as I would love to hear you all stand around and go at it all afternoon, I need to get going. Brother Edwards was the last one out of the church, I believe, and I, umm, I have some business I need to take care of."

All three pairs of eyes focused on Terrance. He got a temporary reprieve when his secretary, Raquel Mason, stuck her head out the sanctuary door.

"Pastor, I've wrapped everything up," she said, smiling when she saw the three women. "Hello, ladies." They all smiled back as they spoke.

"Will you be needing anything else?" Raquel asked.

"No, thank you," Terrance responded.

"Okay, I have to get home and fix dinner for Dolan."

"When are you gonna get that fiancé of yours to come to church?" Terrance asked.

"When hell freezes over," Mamie mumbled. Eva pushed her arm to get her to shut up.

Raquel either didn't hear her or chose to ignore her. "I'm working on it, Pastor. But you know how it is."

Terrance didn't press the issue because he knew that it was a sore spot with his faithful secretary. It hurt his heart to see the pain in her eyes when she talked about the man she was set to marry in less than five months. But she would never really open up to Terrance about it, so there wasn't much he could do.

"Well, you all have a blessed day. I parked out back." Raquel waved as she walked back inside the church.

She had barely closed the door when Eva turned back to her nephew. "Now, back to you. What kind of business do you have on a Sunday afternoon other than dinner with us?" Eva was trying not to let her attitude show.

Terrance normally spent Sunday afternoons having dinner and visiting with his aunts. It had broken Eva's heart that he'd gotten his own place when he moved back to Houston. The only thing that soothed her was that it wasn't far from her.

"I just have something I need to take care of," Terrance softly responded. Even though he was twenty-nine years old and an esteemed pastor, his aunts still had a way of making him feel like a little boy.

"I know you ain't got a date you haven't told us about," Mamie said.

Terrance bit his lip. He knew at some point in his life he was going to have to cut the apron strings his aunts had tied firmly around his neck. "For your information, I do."

"With who?" all three women asked in unison.

"I don't know why you all feel like my dates need your stamp of approval," Terrance said, trying not to let his frustrations show.

He didn't date much and had never brought anyone home to meet his family. It's not that he couldn't get women. On the contrary, he never had a hard time attracting women. Truthfully, he just had a lot of demons he was dealing with, so a serious relationship wasn't on his radar. And the few women he met that he did like could never measure up to the "Lily Grove" standard anyway.

"Now, Terrance, that is so unfair of you to act like we don't want you to find a woman," Eva said. "Remember, I tried to set you up with Sister Eloise's daughter."

Terrance caught himself from rolling his eyes. "Yeah, the girl with the stuttering problem. Look, I don't want to have this conversation again. If and when it looks like this date is going anywhere, I'll bring her home to meet you all. Until then"—he leaned in and kissed each woman gently on the cheek—"get you some business and stay out of mine." He smiled widely, while they narrowed their eyes in disapproval.

"I know, I know"—he laughed as he walked off—"as if that would ever happen."

chapter 2

I really hate dating, Terrance thought as he sat and listened to his blind date ramble on about her supposed modeling career. She had not once stopped to ask him how his day had gone, or anything about himself for that matter.

Terrance had reluctantly given in when Monty, his best friend from college, claimed to have "the perfect woman" for him. Terrance should've known if Monty had anything to do with it, she was a perfect ten and that was about it. She was absolutely gorgeous. Tall, thin, and shapely, caramel-colored skin, and a Colgate smile. But looks were about all she had going for her.

"So, what do you think? Should I get blond highlights or bronze highlights?" she asked as she ran her fingers through her long locks.

Terrance looked at her, confused. "Excuse me?"

She playfully reached across the table and slapped his hand. "Silly, I was talking about my hair. I want to do something different for the modeling shoot I have next week. It's just a catalog, but did you know Naomi

Campbell started in catalog modeling? So it's really just a springboard for me like it was for her."

Terrance took a sip of his iced tea, then glanced at his watch. "Wow, we've only been here twenty minutes."

She giggled. "I know, time is just flying by."

Terrance flashed a fake smile. He didn't realize he'd said that out loud. For him, the twenty minutes felt like hours.

The waitress came and set their food in front of them. Terrance took that as an opportunity to try to change the focus of their conversation. "So, did Monty tell you I'm a minister?"

"Get outta here. Naw, he failed to mention that. I ain't never been on a date with a preacher man before. No wonder you wouldn't have a martini with me." She raised her glass.

Terrance finally displayed a genuine smile. "No, I do have a drink every now and then, but I especially don't drink on Sundays."

She sipped her martini, then seductively bit into the olive. "Shoot, I'll drink any day of the week. It don't matter to me what day it is. Besides, didn't Jesus used to love him some wine?"

Terrance was just about to say something when he looked up to see Savannah standing over his table.

"Hi, Pastor," she said with a surprised smile.

"Well, hello, Sister Savannah. And who might this be?" He motioned toward the young girl standing next to Savannah. She had long crochet braids, a sleeveless tank top, and some skin-tight blue jeans. She wore a scowl across her face, and her arms were folded defiantly across her chest.

Savannah lost her smile. "This would be Misha. She's my Little Sister."

Terrance's eyebrows raised. "Oh, I didn't know you had any sisters."

"She's not my real sister. We're in the Big Sisters program. I'm supposed to be mentoring her, but as you can see, it can prove quite challenging." Savannah forced a small smile.

"That's because I told you I don't want to come up in this ol' fancy restaurant," Misha snapped. "Why couldn't we go to Timmy Chan's or somethin' and get some wings?"

"I told you, because I want you to be exposed to some finer things in life." Savannah sighed.

"Whatever," Misha said, rolling her eyes.

Terrance's date loudly cleared her throat.

"Oh, I'm so sorry. Where are my manners?" Terrance motioned across the table. "Savannah, this is Nadia. Nadia, Savannah attends church with me."

Nadia didn't bother to hide her displeasure. "We were in the middle of dinner, you know."

"Oh, I'm sorry," Savannah said. "Pastor, I just saw you and wanted to come say hello."

Nadia waved her off. "Well, you said it, so now you and the little juvenile delinquent can keep going."

"No, you didn't," Misha snapped, rolling her neck. "You don't know nothing about me."

Savannah gently put her hand on Misha's arm, trying to keep the girl from going off. "Misha, we talked about keeping your anger under control."

"Then, you'd betta tell this tramp not to be disrespecting me." Misha wiggled her finger toward Nadia.

"*Tramp?* Little girl, I will beat you like your mama should've been beating you years ago." Nadia threw her napkin down on the table and stood up.

"Nadia!" Terrance admonished. "She's a child."

"I ain't no child," Misha screamed. "I'm fourteen and I ain't scared of nobody!"

This time Savannah grabbed Misha's arm with a lot more force. "Misha, calm yourself down, girl! What have I told you about how a lady acts? A lady doesn't have to resort to fighting, name-calling, or acting a fool—especially in a public place."

Savannah's words must've gotten to Misha, because the teen backed down. She looked like she wanted to say something else, but she just rolled her eyes at Nadia instead. Savannah smiled. "Good job. I'm proud of you," she softly said, before turning back to Terrance. "Again, I apologize for interrupting your dinner."

Terrance stared at Nadia, trying not to let his disgust show. "Don't apologize, Savannah," he said, his eyes still glued to Nadia. "We were just wrapping up anyway."

"No, we weren't," Nadia snapped as she sat back down in her seat.

"Pastor, I'll see you on Sunday." Savannah took Misha's hand and led her across the restaurant.

Terrance pulled his wallet out.

"I said, we aren't finished with dinner." Nadia glared at him.

"Yes. We are." Terrance pulled out enough money to pay for the meal, then politely stood. "Thank you so much for dinner. I would like to say it's been a pleasure, but it hasn't been."

"Oh, so you're mad because I didn't let that little ghetto girl talk to me crazy, huh?"

"She's a child."

Nadia threw up a hand as she reached down and picked up her glass. "She needs to act like one then." She sipped the rest of her drink.

"Have a good night." Terrance shook his head as he made his way out of the restaurant. As he waited on the valet to bring his car around, Terrance pulled out his cell phone to call Monty and let him know that there would absolutely be no more blind dates.

chapter 3

Terrance stared in disbelief at the perfectly shaped figure in front of him. He had to blink several times to make sure he wasn't seeing things. When he deduced that he wasn't, he said, "Zinetta, put your clothes back on."

Zinetta locked the bathroom door and slithered toward him. "Come on, Pastor. Don't tell me I'm not turning you on."

He took in her body, which was healthy and perfectly toned. Her short, feathered haircut made her look like a lighter version of the actress Gabrielle Union. Of course she turned him on, but her being completely naked in the men's restroom of the Hyatt Hotel also turned him off. Monty might jump for joy at the sight of a naked woman trying to seduce him in a public restroom. But for Terrance, it was disgusting, especially because the scholarship banquet was taking place right in the room next door. Terrance was the keynote speaker for the banquet, held by Calvary Baptist Church. He'd taken a moment during dinner to run to the restroom. Did

Zinetta really think he was about to get it on with her in the men's bathroom?

"Zinetta, I will ask you again. Please put your clothes back on."

A confused look crossed Zinetta's face. "I . . . I don't understand."

"What's not to understand?" Terrance asked as he reached down to pick up her dress and underwear, which she had discarded at the door. "I want you to put your clothes back on." He handed the clothes to her.

"B . . . But Gwen said you were in here waiting on me. She told me how she overheard you telling Brother Baker that it was your ultimate fantasy to have me in a public place." Zinetta took her clothes from Terrance and covered up her private parts. Her butterscotch skin was turning crimson. "I would've never done something like this. But Gwen said you liked aggressive women."

Terrance let out a long sigh. "Gwen as in Tongela's friend Gwen?"

"Well, yeah." Zinetta closed her eyes as realization set in. "That witch."

Terrance suddenly felt bad for her. He couldn't believe Tongela had set Gwen up to do that. Well, yes, he could. Tongela and Zinetta had been rivals for his affection for months. Truthfully, he didn't care for either of them.

"Just put your clothes back on, Zinetta. I'm going back into the program."

Zinetta slipped her dress over her head. "I hope you don't think bad of me, Pastor. I was just—"

Terrance cut her off. "Don't worry about it." He'd become used to the women of his church—and every church within a fifty-mile radius—throwing themselves at him. As one of the only single, black male ministers in the city of Houston, he'd become a prime target for the husband-stalkers. If he had a dime for every time someone had tried to fix him up or come on to him, he'd be a rich man.

He had politely shunned most of the women who had all but thrown themselves at him. They just didn't capture his interest. Well, that excluded Savannah. He didn't quite know what it was about her, but something inside him wanted to get to know her better.

Terrance walked out of the bathroom and back toward the ballroom. He saw Tongela and Gwen snickering over in a corner as they watched the bathroom.

"Evening, Reverend Ellis," Tongela called out.

"That was foul, Tongela. And you know it," Terrance responded as he stopped in front of the two.

Tongela was just about to say something when Zinetta came racing out of the bathroom like a crazed woman. "You tramp! I'm 'bout sick of you!"

Terrance grabbed her just as she clawed at Tongela. The attack caught Tongela off guard, but only for a minute, because she quickly began to attack back.

"Don't be mad at me cuz you're a ho! Like he would want you anyway!" She swung wildly at Zinetta, hitting both Terrance and Zinetta on the side of the head.

Two other men who were walking out of the ballroom noticed the brewing fight and came rushing over. By that time, Terrance was smack-dead in the middle of a girl fight.

It only took about five minutes to get the women under control, but it seemed like an eternity.

"Sir, we're escorting the ladies out," said a security guard who had come upstairs in the midst of the chaos. "Can you come to our office and give us a report of what happened?"

Terrance sighed deeply. He had never been so embarrassed. The program had all but stopped as everyone stood around staring.

"I'm sorry, sir," Terrance responded, "but I'm here to deliver a speech. I'm not involved in what happened here. I was just trying to break it up. I can talk to you after the banquet, but right now, I'd like us to refocus on the reason why we're here. Now, please excuse me."

Terrance held his head up as he made his way back in the banquet room. Thankfully, a lot of people were there. Maybe no one would piece together that the two women fighting were from his church.

He took a quick gulp of water after returning to his seat at the head table. He needed to settle down—and fast—because these women were getting completely out of control.

chapter 4

Terrance took a deep breath and tried not to let his frustrations show. "Brother Baker, we have gone back and forth about you and this bickering and name-calling. Now this is my last warning."

Carl Baker, one of the longtime deacons at Lily Grove, didn't try to hide his scowl. "Well, tell that old battle-ax to stop interrupting me."

Mamie stood up. Her white hair hung limply on her shoulders. Her turquoise blue dress draped her size eighteen frame. "Who are you calling a battle-ax? Don't make me get ugly in the Lord's house. I will take off my wig and beat your—"

"Aunt Mamie!" Terrance snapped. "I know you're not about to go there."

Mamie glared at Carl, poked out her lips, and sat back down. "This fool 'bout to make me lose my religion," she muttered.

Terrance let out a long sigh. "This is getting ridiculous. We're in the midst of getting a new building. Our church is growing by leaps and bounds. We're getting new members every church service, and yet, we're dealing with the same old problems."

"That's cuz you got the same ol' battle-axes trying to run things," Carl spat.

"One mo', Carl. Just one mo' time you call me out of my name and it's on," Mamie threatened.

Terrance slammed his palm down on the large conference-room table. "Enough! I said." He turned to his aunt. "Aunt Mamie, you know I love you, but I will put you out of this business meeting. You and Brother Baker," he added, glaring at Carl. "Now, I will ask you for the last time, be quiet and refrain from name-calling."

Mamie rolled her eyes. Carl leaned back in his chair and crossed his arms defiantly.

"Now, where were we?" Terrance said, looking at his agenda. These business meetings were getting more and more stressful, particularly because Carl and his aunt mixed like oil and water.

Raquel, who was sitting next to Terrance, reached over and pointed at the fifth item on his agenda. "We were discussing some new ideas for the youth."

"And as I was saying, before I was so rudely interrupted," Mamie continued, "I think we should start a mentoring group for the young people, but I think we should open it up to the surrounding community."

"And I still say, we're not in the business of caring for juvenile delinquents," Carl interjected.

"It would be a great way to get some of these kids off the streets," Mamie added, ignoring Carl.

"I don't know, Mamie," Eva said skeptically. "Why

can't we just do it for our youth here at the church? Why should we open it up to the public?"

"Because our youth here at Lily Grove are pretty much on the straight and narrow, and we need to help others who aren't," Mamie replied.

"Don't they have a youth program like that at Zion Hill?" Raquel asked.

Mamie nodded as she reached down in her bag and pulled out a photocopy of a newspaper article. "Ummm-hmmm. They call it the Good Girlz, and I've heard such wonderful things about it. We're always talking about looking at ways to bring more young people into the church. I think this is a way to do it." She pushed the paper toward Terrance.

Carl continued to shake his head. "Y'all ain't gon' be happy till some teenager done stole the stereo system," he mumbled.

Terrance decided to ignore Carl as well as he glanced over the article. "You know, I think that's an excellent idea, Aunt Mamie. A church is more than just the four walls. A church that's truly serving of God goes out into the community and does good as well."

Mamie smiled triumphantly.

"And I have just the person to lead the group." Terrance took a deep breath and flashed a wide grin. "Sister Savannah would be perfect to head up something like that."

The room grew silent. Mamie's smile slowly faded.

"Excuse me." Eva cocked her head to the side. "Who did you say?"

Terrance thought back to Savannah and the young girl she was with. He'd only been around them a short time, but he could tell Savannah was making a difference in the teen's life. He'd truly been impressed with the passion Savannah seemed to show toward the girl.

"I said, Savannah McKinney," Terrance repeated.

"Flo's granddaughter Savannah?" Mamie asked with an incredulous look across her face.

"Yes. And what's wrong with her?" Terrance knew the answer, but for some reason he was hoping they would give Savannah a chance.

Eva leaned in like she was studying her nephew, trying to see if he was serious. "Terrance, you've got to be kidding, right? Savannah McKinney is not the type of woman we'd want being associated with this church in any shape, form, or fashion."

Terrance knew people around Lily Grove didn't particularly care for Savannah, but he did always like her spunky personality. And seeing her with Misha allowed him to see her in a whole new light, one that really impressed him. "You still haven't told me, what is wrong with Savannah?" Terrance asked. "Something based on fact and not church-house rumors."

"Fact is, she's a ho," Mamie mumbled.

"Aunt Mamie!" Terrance snapped.

Mamie put her hand to her mouth. "Oops, did I say that out loud? Sorry, she's a garden tool."

"You don't know anything about her, other than the rumors that circulate around this church," Terrance admonished.

"Maybe not," Mamie said. "But I do know that where there's smoke, there's fire. And Savannah McKinney got a cloud full of smoke surrounding her."

Dorothy Mae, who'd been sitting quietly at the end

of the table, finally spoke up. Her voice was steady, like she was trying to be reasonable. "Terrance, Mamie could have found a better choice of words, but as Eva said, she's just not the one to lead the young people here at Lily Grove. Don't we have another member who'd be more fitting?"

Terrance debated saying more to his aunts, because he really hated the way people treated Savannah. She seemed like a really sweet girl, whom no one bothered to give a chance. But judging from the looks at the table, no one would be trying to hear anything he had to say.

"How about we just table this issue for now," Terrance said, glancing at his watch. "It's getting late and I know we're all tired."

Several people nodded in agreement. Everyone stood and said their respective good-byes. Terrance glanced down at the newspaper article, loving Mamie's idea more by the minute. His thoughts raced back to Savannah. They'd never go for the idea of her leading the youth group, but Terrance found himself intrigued, wanting to know more about her.

Maybe I won't call Savannah to lead the youth group, Terrance thought, but now more than ever he was sure of one thing: he was definitely going to call her.

chapter 5

Eva held her arm out to quiet her sisters. They'd just spent two hours at the church for a budget meeting and had returned to help Dorothy Mae find her beloved brooch, which had fallen off sometime during the evening.

They were heading toward the conference room when Eva spotted Deacon Raymond Tisdale easing into the room.

"I thought everyone was gone," Mamie said.

Eva waved to shut her up. Deacon Tisdale's shysty behind definitely didn't look like he was up to any good. "I heard him tell Terrance he had to get home right after the meeting, so what is he doing back here looking all sneaky?" Eva whispered.

"I suggest we go see, because there goes Louis Allen going in the conference room as well," Dorothy Mae responded.

"I know they're not trying to have some type of private meeting without Terrance," Eva snapped. She tried to stay back and let Terrance run the church how he saw fit, but she wasn't about to have the deacons doing something behind Terrance's back. And if they were having some type of private meeting, they were definitely up to no good.

"Only one way to find out," Dorothy Mae said, as she pushed her way past Eva and down the long hall.

The other two women followed her. All three of them stopped right outside the conference room door, which was cracked open.

"Now, Raymond, I'm not saying I don't like the boy. Shoot, I think he's a pretty good preacher. But he is 'bout to be thirty years old and ain't got no wife or even a steady girlfriend," a voice Eva recognized as Carl Baker's said.

"And you know folks have started whispering that maybe he's one of them DL ministers," Louis interjected. "Now y'all know I don't like gossip, but let me tell you what I heard. A reliable source told me that Zinetta Chambers got butt naked as a jaybird the other day and cornered Reverend Ellis in a hotel bathroom. And do you know what he did?"

"What?" several of the men asked.

"Absolutely nothing," Louis said, like Terrance had committed a cardinal sin. "Told that pretty young thang to put her clothes back on and get out."

"You lying," someone interjected.

"If I'm lying, I'm flying," Louis said. "Plus, y'all know he was counseling them two gay fellas from the choir."

"So he ain't supposed to counsel certain people because of their sexuality?" Dorothy Mae whispered. Eva waved her hand for her sister to be quiet.

"And you know he's always hanging around with that Monty fella," Carl said.

"Come to think of it, that Monty ain't never been married either, huh?" Deacon Tisdale asked.

"Nope, though I did hear he got some gal on the North Side pregnant," Carl responded.

"It probably was a cover-up," Deacon Tisdale said.

"So y'all really think the boy is gay?" Carl asked.

Eva had to clutch her heart with one hand and use the other to grab hold of Dorothy Mae, who looked ready to charge into the meeting. Terrance and Monty were roommates in college, and Monty was really the only guy Terrance hung out with. But he was a busy preacher, Eva thought. He didn't have time to be hanging out with a bunch of folks. That the deacons were trying to read more into his relationship was troubling.

"All I'm saying is, we got the big hundred-year Christmas service coming up in less than four months, and we got five churches that will be here visiting," Louis said, clearly agitated. "That's five ministers, and guess what? Every single one of them will have a first lady on their arms."

"So, Reverend Ellis gon' have the first man on his arm?" another deacon joked.

"Bruce, this is serious. We ain't got no time for jokes," Deacon Tisdale admonished. "Now, I been understanding for the longest, but I'm starting to wonder. I don't want our church made a fool of at the biggest event this church has ever seen."

"Why don't we just talk to Pastor?" someone asked.

"For what? So he can go run out and get him a decoy? If the boy is gay, I want to know about it now," Carl barked.

"He ain't gay," another deacon, Phil Wilson, responded. "I just don't think he's found Mrs. Right."

Louis huffed, "Well, what kind of church are we with no first lady? Folks bound to talk. Shoot, the first lady is supposed to host the Christmas breakfast. We been having them old biddies do it since Terrance took over as pastor three years ago. It's been fine because it ain't been nobody but us, but now that we're expecting five times as many people, we need to be properly represented."

"Well, what do you suppose we do?" Carl asked.

Deacon Tisdale huffed. "I don't know. It may be too late to do anything, but I do know this—if that Christmas service rolls around here and he's still single, then we need to start asking ourselves is there something a little more low-down that we need to be concerning ourselves with."

Eva couldn't believe her ears. Not only were they insinuating that her baby was gay, but then they had the nerve to be thinking about firing him.

Eva felt sick to her stomach. She'd spent her life trying to keep Terrance on the straight and narrow, and despite the bumpy youth he had, she was proud of how he turned out.

"I can't stand anyone messing up my baby's good name," Eva mumbled.

"So what are we gonna do about it?" Dorothy Mae asked.

Eva glanced toward the conference room door. "We're goin' to find our baby a woman, and we're goin' to do it in time for the Christmas celebration," Eva proclaimed.

chapter 6

Terrance wiped the sweat from his brow. He was pleased. As usual, he'd delivered a spirit-rousing sermon.

"Let the church say amen," Terrance said as the choir began singing.

"Amen," the congregation replied.

"I know someone out there is wrestling with something. I'm here to tell you, don't worry about it. Pray about it. Come now, bring it to the Lord." Terrance stretched out his arms.

He smiled as he looked at Savannah in the second row, her eyes closed as she swayed gently to the sounds of the choir. She opened her eyes and he noticed that they were filled with tears.

"The battle is not yours, it's the Lord's," Terrance continued as he kept his eyes on Savannah. She inhaled deeply, then stood and made her way to the front.

Several eyes were fixed on Savannah as she walked up the aisle. She kept her gaze focused straight ahead.

Terrance waited a few more minutes before turning the microphone over to Raquel, who had been logging the names of the people who came to the altar.

"Giving honor to God, Reverend Ellis, members, and friends," Raquel began, "we have six people who come to join by Christian experience, and one person"—she motioned toward Savannah—"who comes for prayer."

Terrance didn't know what, in particular, Savannah wanted prayer for, but he was pleased to see her come to the front.

He said a few words to the congregation before offering up a prayer for Savannah.

After he'd dismissed church and said his good-byes to the members, Terrance found himself looking around for Savannah. He wanted to talk to her privately and make sure everything was all right.

"Hey, Brother Edwards," Terrance said when he noticed Chester picking up discarded programs in the sanctuary. "Have you seen Savannah McKinney around here anywhere? She didn't come out through the front and I was hoping to speak with her."

"Umph, I bet you were hoping to speak with her. I bet you was hopin' for a whole lot more." Chester chuckled.

Terrance shot him a chastising look. "Now, now, Brother Edwards, get your mind out of the gutter."

"Come on, Pastor. Ain't nothing to be ashamed of. That's one fine young thang there."

"Have you seen her?" Terrance asked, trying to ignore the dirty look on Chester's face.

"Umm-hmmm. I saw her in the hallway in the back

by the ladies' room. Her equally fine grandmother was back there with her."

Terrance shook his head as he walked off laughing. "Thanks."

"Don't do nothin' I wouldn't do," Chester called out.

Terrance waved him off as he headed through the sanctuary to the back hall to the ladies' restroom. He had just turned the corner when he saw Savannah standing with her head lowered. Her grandmother stood over her, wagging her finger. Savannah looked like a child being scolded by her parents.

"You're just pathetic. How you gon' let them women sit up there and talk about you like that?" Flo said.

Savannah didn't respond.

"You gon' learn. These people around this church ain't nothin' but hypocrites."

"Then what do you come for?"

"To get under their skin." Flo blew a frustrated breath. "I would've slapped that woman into next week if I was in a bathroom stall while she was talking about me like a dog. But what do you do? You come running out of the bathroom like a little girl. Crying like you crazy. They talked about Jesus. You think they ain't gon' talk about you? Especially because they jealous."

Savannah dabbed at her eyes. "I told you, I was just upset because I didn't do anything to these women, and I was mad that they were talking about how Terrance would never want a woman like me."

"He won't. But I told you that already. You need to get off that pipe dream. You're good for one thing and one thing only with him, and that's a romp in the hay. And quiet as it's kept, ain't nothing wrong with that. As long as at the end of the day, he's the one who got used. You use men before they use you," Flo warned again.

Terrance could no longer stomach the horrible things Flo was saying. He walked toward them to make his presence known.

Savannah's eyes immediately grew wide. Flo looked like she could care less whether he'd heard her or not.

"Good afternoon, ladies," Terrance said as he approached them. "How are you all today?"

"I'm fine," Savannah said.

Flo didn't respond. She just kept her arms crossed and looked him up and down.

"Well, Sister Savannah, I was just looking for you. I was hoping, well, I would like it if you would have dinner with me."

Savannah's eyes widened again—but this time with delight. Shock registered all over Flo's face.

"Dinner for what?" Flo interjected.

Terrance let out a small laugh. "Dinner to eat."

"I would like that," Savannah interjected before her grandmother could say anything else.

"Do you want me to come pick you up, or do you just want to meet me back up here at six?"

The sadness was gone from Savannah's face. Now, she looked giddy. "I'll be here at six."

Flo huffed like she thought Terrance's request was some type of scam. "You remember what I told you," she said as she walked off. "You can't trust none of 'em!"

Terrance ignored Flo. "Great, I'll see you at six here at the church." Terrance hadn't really planned to ask

Savannah out right then and there, but watching Flo give her a hard time just caused his basic protector instincts to kick in. But more than anything, Terrance found himself asking Savannah out because there was something about her that he was just ready to know better.

chapter 7

Raquel stood in the arched doorway of Terrance's office, staring at him strangely.

"What?" Terrance asked, looking up from his desk.

"I'm just wondering why you're sitting here at your desk in an empty room, smiling like a crazy person."

A lopsided smile crossed his face. "I didn't realize I was sitting here smiling." He closed the church budget notes he'd been poring over before his mind started to drift to Savannah.

"You weren't smiling. You were cheesing," Raquel joked as she walked in and stood in front of his desk. "You wanna tell me what gives?"

Terrance debated for a moment. He was feeling like a little boy with his first crush after talking on the phone with Savannah two nights ago for almost three hours. He couldn't remember the last time he'd talked to a woman that long, and enjoyed it. They continued their conversation over dinner yesterday.

He'd broken down and asked her for feedback on the youth project. Of course, she had been gung ho on the idea and had even suggested herself to lead the group. Terrance told her they were just in the planning stages and would get back to her later. Between their date and their phone call, they'd begun talking about everything under the sun. Savannah had a great sense of humor, and Terrance found himself laughing like he hadn't laughed in a long time. In fact, his mind had started drifting because it was almost six o'clock and Savannah was picking him up from the church so they could go out again. Of course, he didn't like the idea of her picking him up, but she'd been adamant that since tonight's date was her suggestion, he allow her to take charge. That was another thing he liked about her, she wasn't the typical demure "Whatever you say, Pastor" type of woman he had dated over the last few years. No, Savannah marched to her own drum and he liked that.

"Oh, it's no big deal. I'm just in a good mood," Terrance finally said. He didn't feel completely comfortable discussing his love life with his secretary.

"Ummm-hmmm." Raquel nodded skeptically. "That's a new-woman look if I ever seen one. But if you don't want to tell me who it is, I understand." She feigned a look like she was hurt.

Terrance smiled. "What may I help you with today? Since I know you didn't come in here to talk about my love life."

"See, I knew that's what it was." Raquel laughed. "Actually, I'm probably about to spoil your good mood."

"How?" Terrance asked, his eyebrows narrowing.

"Your aunts are outside. They look secretive and agitated. I don't know what's going on, but they told me to let you know they'd be waiting for you out back."

"Waiting for me for what?" Terrance stood up, looked at his watch, then let out an exasperated breath. Savannah was going to meet him out back in less than five minutes. The last thing he wanted was his aunts to be anywhere around. "What do they want? I really don't feel like dealing with them today."

"I don't know what they want." Raquel shrugged. "And don't raise your voice at me. I'm just the messenger."

Terrance let a small smile form on his lips. "Sorry."

"Ummm-hmmm," Raquel said as she walked back to the door. "I told you I was going to make you lose that smile."

Terrance leaned over and shut off his computer. Maybe if he could get back there, he could see what they wanted, then get rid of them before Savannah arrived.

"Thanks for bringing the message," Terrance said. "I'm going to head out. I'll see you tomorrow."

Raquel bid him good-bye as he made his way down the long hallway and out the back door. All three of his aunts stood around on the steps, like they were engrossed in a deep conversation.

"Ladies," Terrance said, "what can I help you all with today? Is this about yesterday's budget meeting?"

Eva spun around. Terrance expected to see her face light up as it normally did whenever he entered a room. Instead she had a worried look.

"Hi, sweetheart. How are you?" Eva's voice lacked the warmth it normally held.

Terrance lost his smile. "I'm fine." He looked toward Mamie, then Dorothy Mae. "Wondering what's going on with you all, why you're standing out here looking so serious."

Eva sighed, then took a step toward Terrance. She gently ran her hand along his cheek. "We're just worried about you, that's all."

Terrance frowned up. He didn't like where this was headed. "Worried about me for what?"

"We just want you to be happy," Dorothy Mae added, stepping up next to him. "A fine young man like yourself shouldn't be alone."

Terrance let out a laugh. "I should've known that that's what this was about. My aunts, always trying to find me a woman."

"You're an esteemed minister. You need a good woman by your side," Eva chimed in.

"I've told you all a hundred times, when it's time for me to find a woman, I will. I don't need . . ." His voice trailed off as he looked toward the curb and at the convertible SAAB that came to a screeching halt in back of the church.

Eva, Dorothy Mae, and Mamie all turned in unison to look at the car. The wild-haired woman threw the car in park and pulled herself up on the seat.

"Hey, handsome, you ready to roll?" she called out to Terrance.

"Good Lord Almighty," Eva muttered. "Is that Savannah McKinney?" she asked in disbelief.

"Yep, it's the hoochie mama," Mamie mumbled. "As if you could mistake that wild honey blond hair and double-D breasts."

Terrance let out a long sigh. "Savannah is not a hoochie mama."

Both Dorothy Mae and Mamie turned up their noses. "Oh, yes, she is," Mamie snapped. "She's a hoochie mama, her mama is a hoochie mama, and her mama's mama is a hoochie mama."

"Um-hmm, that Savannah is just like her grandma, been with everybody under the sun. Everyone knows that," Dorothy Mae added. "And she's definitely not the type of woman you need to be associating with."

"How are you ladies doing this evening?" Savannah called out. None of the women responded. Savannah shrugged indifferently and kept her smile plastered on. "T-baby, are you ready?"

" 'T-baby'?" Eva hissed, turning to Terrance. "Does she know you're a highly regarded minister and not some thug off the street?"

Terrance sighed. Savannah *had* gone a little overboard with the entrance, but he would have to talk to her about that later. Right now, he just wanted to get away.

He leaned in and kissed Eva on the cheek. "Gotta go."

"Terrance Deshaun Ellis, I know you are not about to be seen getting into that car with that floozy," Mamie snapped as she looked around nervously.

Terrance debated saying anything, then figured, what was the use? "Bye, ladies," he said, then lightly kissed Mamie and Dorothy Mae on the cheek. "I'll call you later." He headed to Savannah's car before they could say another word.

All three of the women watched him get in the car with Savannah, who quickly tried to lean over and kiss him. Terrance gently pushed her away, knowing seeing Savannah kiss him would only set his aunts off even more.

"Awww, hell no," Mamie muttered.

Eva swatted her sister's shoulder. "Mamie. You're standing on the Lord's ground. Stop using that foul language."

"In this case, I think God understands," Mamie mumbled.

The women watched the car until it turned the corner. They stood in silence for a few minutes. "Ladies, it is definitely time," Eva muttered, still shaking her head.

"Time for what?" Dorothy Mae asked.

"Time to find that boy a wife," Eva replied. "Because Savannah McKinney is not the answer."

Dorothy Mae turned to Eva and nodded. "For once, big sister, I couldn't agree with you more."

chapter 8

Terrance felt a smile creep across his face as he watched Savannah. Her hair was long and untamed, but it looked so sexy on her. She was dressed a little too provocatively for his taste with her white, tight tank top and tight Apple Bottoms jeans. Still, he had to admit that she looked gorgeous.

Savannah was animated as she described some of the stuff Misha, her Little Sister, had gotten into.

". . . and she climbed in the boy's window and jumped him and the girl he was cheating on her with," Savannah said, shaking her head. "I tell you, that girl keeps my hands full." Savannah ran her finger across the top of her glass of wine as her laughter died down.

"What?" she said, when she noticed Terrance continuing to stare at her. "Why are you looking at me like that?"

Terrance leaned back in his chair as the light sounds of jazz filled the air. They were on the covered patio of the Wonder Bar, an upscale jazz bar/restaurant in downtown Houston. Savannah had assured him that he would love the atmosphere. She was right. He was a connoisseur of jazz music, and he appreciated that Savannah had done her homework to find that out.

"I'm just listening," Terrance replied. "I love how vibrant you seem to become when you're talking about Misha."

Savannah matched his smile, a hint of bashfulness creeping up. "Yeah, Misha brings me a lot of joy. She really is a good kid, she just doesn't have anyone in her life who cares about her. Her dad was shot and killed in a drug deal. And her mom runs the streets all the time. So she pretty much fends for herself." Savannah brushed her hair out of her face as she leaned back in her chair. "I guess that's why I'm so attached to her."

Terrance continued to take in Savannah's beauty as she talked. There was no denying her outward beauty, but the more he talked to her, the more he was becoming enamored with what was inside. "So you feel a sort of kindred spirit with her?" Terrance asked.

Savannah nodded, her smile fading. "I guess you can call it that." She sighed. "You know I was raised by my grandmother, right?"

Terrance had known both Savannah and her grandmother since they started going to Lily Grove about three years ago. "Yeah, Sister Florence."

"Good old Grandma Flo." Savannah frowned slightly before continuing, "The woman who never wanted a kid and dang sure didn't want a grandkid. She reminded me of that every chance she got."

Terrance knew Flo treated Savannah poorly, but judging from the pain etched across Savannah's face, they had some deep-rooted issues.

"It's hard to believe your own grandmother could be like that toward you," Terrance said.

"Trust me. My grandmother is far from your typical grandmother." Savannah let out a pained laugh. "You'll never catch her baking cookies, showering anyone with love, or any grandmotherly thing at all for that matter."

"Where's your mother?" Terrance found himself wanting to know more about Savannah, especially this side of her that seemed so full of hurt.

Savannah turned up her lips. "Mother? What's that?" She shook her head as her eyes began to mist. "I was a mistake. The result of a night of too much drinking and partying. My mother didn't even know where to start in looking for my father. So, when I was born, she told me I was cramping her style, dumped me with my grandmother, and took off. I see her every now and then when she blows through town, and one time she stayed sober long enough for us to even have a conversation. And my grandmother wasn't much better. She ran through men like it was nothing. That's my legacy."

She held up her glass and took a long swig, then dabbed at her eyes. "This wine has me all emotional, blabbing all my business. Don't pay me any attention." She took a deep breath, trying to compose herself.

Terrance stared in amazement. "Wow. I'm sorry to hear that."

"Don't be." She sighed. "I got over it a long time ago."

They sat in silence for a few minutes and listened to the jazz band. Terrance could tell Savannah was deep in thought. Just from the little she'd told him, he could tell that she had had a hard life. Something about watching her made him want to take her into his arms and protect her from the world.

"Thanks for coming out tonight," the lead singer in the band said, interrupting Terrance's thoughts. "We're going to take a brief intermission and then come right back up to bring you some more sweet jazz sounds."

They both joined in applauding the band as more jazz filled the sound system in the restaurant.

Terrance leaned in and took Savannah's hand as the band members exited the stage. "So tell me, why are you still single?"

Savannah chuckled. "I've been asking myself that for the last five years." She motioned toward the waiter and pointed toward her glass.

"Another glass coming right up," the waiter replied.

Savannah crossed her legs and sighed. "My grandmother says love is a figment of people's imagination. Ain't no such thing, she loves to spout. I know she's jaded. My grandfather—the only man she's ever confessed to loving—left her when he found out she was pregnant. I think that really messed her up."

"That's really sad."

"Yep, and so now, my grandmother believes men are to be used and discarded."

Terrance stared at her intensely. "Is that what you believe?"

Sadness spread across Savannah's face. "I guess I read too many fairy tales growing up. I believe in true love and I'm hopeful that I will find it."

Terrance squeezed her hand again. "I'm confident that you will, too." *Maybe you already have,* Terrance thought as he smiled.

chapter 9

Terrance squinted, trying to make out the shadowy figure standing in the church parking lot. It was still fairly early—the sun had barely come up so he couldn't see well. It was a man and a woman, and they looked like they were arguing.

Terrance had parked his car around back, but he was going in through the front door because the back-door lock was broken. It could only be secured by dead-bolting the door from the inside. He made a mental note to make sure the locksmith came by the church today.

He walked a little closer to the front, just as the man reached out, grabbed the woman, and slammed her against the car.

"Did that sound like a request to you!" he screamed. "I said, I wanted some eggs and bacon before you left. I don't know who you think you are, but I will—"

"Raquel?" Terrance said, as he finally recognized the woman. "Is everything all right?"

Raquel's tear-filled eyes got wide. She tried to pull away from the man.

"P . . . Pastor. I'm f . . . fine. Good morning." Raquel tried to cover her blouse, which was torn at the top. Her hair was disheveled. "Ummm, this, this is my fiancé, Dolan." She motioned toward the man, who was standing there looking like a pit bull.

Terrance's eyes made their way down to Dolan's hand, which was still firmly gripped around Raquel's arm. "Are you sure you're okay?"

"Didn't you hear her say she was fine?" Dolan growled. "This here is private business between a man and his woman."

"Well, do you really think you should be manhandling her like that?"

Dolan let Raquel's arm drop as he took a couple of steps toward Terrance. "Look here, man—"

"It's Terrance Ellis. Pastor Terrance Ellis."

"Oh, you her boss. The man she always trying to please, while neglecting her duties at home."

Raquel pulled at his arm. "Dolan, please."

He jerked his arm away, keeping his attention focused on Terrance. "You married, Terrance?"

"No, I'm not."

"Close to getting married?"

Terrance shook his head.

"Then it seems like to me you don't know nothing 'bout this here and you'd be better off minding your own business."

Terrance had to remember that he was a God-fearing man, because right about then he wanted to punch this man square in the jaw.

Raquel stepped up. "Pastor, I'm sorry." She turned to her fiancé. "Dolan, please. I'm sorry about breakfast. Can we talk about this when I get home?"

He looked like he debated arguing, but then must've decided it wasn't worth it. "You'd better be glad I'm tired, because I could care less about Jesus over here coming to save the day. All I know is this betta not ever happen again. Ya feel me?"

Raquel slowly nodded.

Dolan shot Terrance one last hateful look before turning and heading to the car. He stopped before getting in the car and looked at Raquel. "And you are right about one thing."

"What?" she softly replied.

"You are sorry." Dolan laughed as he got in the car and sped off.

Terrance stood for a minute, stunned. He would never in a million years have dreamed that Raquel's fiancé would be that cruel. He wasn't even someone he could have imagined with sweet, loving Raquel.

Terrance didn't say anything as he followed Raquel inside the church. He waited until Raquel was settled at her desk, then he took it upon himself to brew some coffee. As soon as it was finished, he poured both of them a cup.

"Just what the doctor ordered," he said, placing the cup on her desk. She still had a distressed look across her face.

"I'm sorry. I would've made that."

Terrance nodded. "I know. I just beat you to the punch. Or rather, the coffee." He held up his cup and laughed at his lame joke.

Raquel finally smiled and took a sip of the coffee. "Thank you." She closed her eyes as if she was enjoying the hot liquid as it slid down her throat.

"Now, you know I couldn't just not say anything, right?" Terrance cupped his coffee in his hands.

"I know that." Raquel opened her eyes and gave him a sly smile. "You wouldn't be Reverend Ellis if you did."

"So"—he took a seat in the chair in front of her desk—"you wanna talk about it?"

The smile left Raquel's face. "Not really. But since I know that answer won't fly with you, I can only say it's not as bad as it seems."

"Really? Because it seemed pretty bad," Terrance said matter-of-factly.

"Dolan gets like that from time to time, mostly after a night of drinking."

"How long have you two been together?"

"Six years."

"You've been dealing with that for six years?" Terrance didn't mean to be so blunt. But there was no use in beating around the bush. What he had just witnessed angered him no end.

Raquel let out a pained laugh. "Really, it hasn't always been like this."

Terrance admired the way Raquel held herself together. He wasn't physically attracted to her, even though she had the most beautiful, smooth cinnamon skin he'd ever seen. She had long, golden brown hair, enchanting light brown eyes, and a smile that lit up the room when she walked in.

"Do you all still live together?" Terrance asked. He wasn't trying to get all in Raquel's business, but he had to ask the question. He hadn't agreed with that when he'd first learned she was moving in with him.

Raquel let out a small groan. "I've told you, we're trying to save money for the wedding. And you know the only relative I have here is my aunt Marjorie, and I can't stay with her or her fifteen cats." She smiled, trying to lighten the mood.

"I know we've been over this a hundred times. I just don't like seeing you give Dolan that much power. You're putting yourself in a position to be totally dependent on him. And if he gets abusive—"

She cut him off. "He's not abusive."

Terrance held up his hand. What he had just witnessed was definitely abuse, but he left that alone. "I'm just saying, if he gets abusive, you have nowhere to go."

"Your concerns are duly noted. Now, can we change the subject?" Raquel took another sip of coffee. "How did your date go with Savannah? Do you think she's the one, or do you need me to find you a backup?"

Terrance laughed as he shook his head. Raquel was also always trying to hook him up. He could tell she didn't particularly care for Savannah, but unlike his aunts, she kept her negative thoughts to herself.

"The date was okay. She's fun to be around. I like her, but as for being the one, I don't know."

"You know the big Christmas program is right around the corner?"

"Trust me, how could I not remember? Rumor on the grapevine is that unless I find a woman by then, I'm getting kicked out."

"Don't be ridiculous. Although I did hear some nonsense along those lines. I think everybody is just anxious for you to find a first lady."

"Well, I wish everybody would just leave me alone and let God send me my wife when He's ready to send me my wife."

"Leave you alone? Please, as long as you're presiding over the great Lily Grove, you know that's not about to happen."

He chuckled. Raquel was definitely right about that.

"Well, right now," Terrance continued, "Savannah is the only prospect on the horizon, and my aunts would just as soon as have me marry Whoopi Goldberg as marry her. But you know what, they'll just have to get over it. Because I'm taking Savannah to dinner this Sunday."

Raquel's mouth dropped open. "Your regular Sunday dinner? At your aunt Eva's?"

Terrance nodded.

"Ooooh, you like drama in your life, don't you?" Raquel teased. "Here." Raquel opened her top desk drawer, reached in, and pulled out a small bottle and handed it to Terrance.

"What's that?"

"Holy oil. You're going to need the whole bottle if you hope to have dinner go off with no problems."

Terrance broke out in laughter as he stood up. "You are crazy."

Raquel couldn't help but smile herself, noticing that despite what he said, he'd taken the bottle and dropped it in his jacket pocket.

chapter 10

Dorothy Mae slammed the pan of macaroni and cheese on the dining room table. The noise made everyone jump. She grunted, then made her way back into the kitchen to get the rest of the food.

"Where's the rat poison? Savannah's asking for sugar," Dorothy Mae snarled. "Messing up my good collard greens with sugar."

"Dorothy Mae, you don't have to make your disdain so obvious," Eva whispered as she pulled more dinner rolls from the oven.

"What you want me to do? Act like I'm happy 'bout that Jezebel sitting up in here?" Dorothy Mae snapped.

"Yeah," Mamie chimed in. "Terrance knows our Sunday dinners have always been us. Why he had to bring her is beyond me."

Eva slyly smiled. "If our dinners are so private, what is Rosolyn doing in there?" Rosolyn was a nurse at the hospital where Mamie used to work until she retired seven years ago.

"Well, I invited her because I knew she'd be all alone today," Mamie replied as she removed another glass from the cabinet. "I thought Terrance, well, if he just gets to know her, I think he'll like her."

"Umph," Eva responded. "I thought we said we would talk about any woman we tried to fix Terrance up with. We were supposed to come up with a list and meet this evening and decide on the top three."

"Well, while y'all busy making up lists, I'm making stuff happen," Mamie said, slamming the cabinet door. "Besides, y'all know Rosolyn."

"But we hadn't agreed on her yet," Dorothy Mae responded.

Mamie rolled her eyes as she walked through the swinging doors and back into the dining room. Two seconds later, she walked right back in the kitchen. "Lord, give me strength."

"What?" Dorothy Mae asked.

"She's running her hand up his leg. At the dinner table! Just shameful," Mamie snapped. "And it's so obvious what she's doing. Terrance is trying to push her hands off of him, but she's like a daggone octopus. And poor Rosolyn is just sitting there horrified."

"No, she's not sitting up there disrespecting my house," Eva said as she pushed her way into the dining room.

"Terrance, may I have a word with you in the kitchen, please?" Eva said, a stern look across her face.

Terrance shook his head, like he knew he was about to venture into territory he didn't feel like treading. He slowly followed Eva into the kitchen. Mamie and Dorothy Mae were standing around the island oven, their arms folded across their chests.

"What is it now, Aunt Eva?" Terrance sighed heavily.

"I think you know what it is," Dorothy Mae snapped. "You are a minister, for Christ's sake. What is wrong with you, letting that floozy paw all over you like that, and at the dinner table at that?"

"I'm not letting her paw all over me. I asked her to stop."

"The fact that she's even doing it at all is sign enough that you don't need to be fooling with her," Mamie piped in. "Why did you even bring her in the first place? You know this is our time."

"Is that so? Then why is Rosolyn here?" Terrance looked around the room. Both Dorothy Mae and Eva looked at Mamie, who shrugged. "I want you all to get to know her better."

"I'm not interested in these women."

"You're not gay, are you, son? I mean, we will love you the same. God might not, but we will," Mamie said, a horrified look across her face. Dorothy Mae slapped her arm. "I'm just being honest," Mamie hissed.

Terrance chuckled as he shook his head. "No, I'm not gay."

"Then what's the problem, baby?" Eva asked, her voice laced with concern. "Why can't you find a good, decent woman?" she added, emphasizing *good* and *decent*. "That's who you need to be looking for while you're wasting your time with Savannah. Can you imagine what people will say if you develop a relationship with that girl?"

"Aunt Eva, you know me well enough to know I just want to spread the word of God to the people. That's it. I'm not interested in the politics, the gossip, or anything else anyone has to say about me."

"But why her?" Mamie looked like she was really trying to make sense of his relationship with Savannah.

Terrance shrugged. "She makes me laugh."

"Watch a comedy video," Dorothy Mae snapped.

Terrance ignored her. "I enjoy spending time with Savannah. Yes, she's a little over-the-top, and a little less refined than most women, but she's really a sweet woman."

"You just caught up. That girl ain't nothin' but trouble," Mamie mumbled, recalling the rumors that had always surrounded Savannah, the latest of which had her being chased out of a motel by Deacon Tisdale's wife.

"Terrance, have you given any thought to the hundred-year Christmas celebration? I mean, I know it's only September, but can you really see yourself having Savannah on your arm at the celebration?" Eva asked matter-of-factly.

"Why do I need to have anyone on my arm?" Terrance exhaled. He was so tired of this debate and even more tired of people trying to run his life. Sometimes, if he had to do it all over again, he might rethink coming back to preach in his hometown church. Between the heavy burden he carried and the people who seemed to make it their business to get all up in his business, Terrance wondered if he'd ever find true happiness.

They'd returned to dinner, but after about twenty minutes, Terrance could tell things weren't going to get any better.

"Well, we'd better get going," he said, picking up his plate.

"Thank you all so much for the wonderful dinner," Savannah offered as she followed Terrance into the kitchen.

"Ummm-hmmm," Eva mumbled. Dorothy Mae and Mamie didn't say anything.

Savannah blew off their nasty attitudes as she walked back in the den and said good-bye to Rosolyn.

Terrance was about to chastise his aunts for their rude behavior, but he changed his mind. However, he knew at some point, if Savannah was going to be in his life, he would have to have a long talk with his aunts.

chapter 11

Savannah walked in and flung her purse across the glass coffee table in her large two-bedroom apartment, which definitely didn't reflect that neither Savannah nor her roommate, Tyra, worked a full-time job. A forty-two-inch television was in the corner. A leather sofa and love seat sat in the middle of the living room. A state-of-the-art stereo system sat in another corner. And all kinds of African art adorned the walls. All of their belongings were compliments of their latest conquests, as well as part of the reason Savannah was ready to settle down. Shoot, trying to survive and keep this man happy long enough to pay her bills, or that man happy long enough to buy her furniture, was a full-time job in itself. The only thing she'd bought with her own money was her used SAAB. And she'd only gotten that after finding out one of the rich guys she was dating was actually married. He'd given her the money for the car just to make her go away. He hadn't even shown any remorse about hurting her. Yep, it was a lifestyle she'd definitely grown weary of.

"What's your problem?" Tyra said as she sat up on the sofa.

Savannah jumped. "Oh, I didn't know you were home. I thought you had a date."

"Please, that sorry fool didn't show. That's the last time he stands me up, that's for sure."

Savannah began removing her earrings as she headed to her bedroom. "That's what you said the last time."

Tyra got up and followed her. "I mean it this time. This is getting really old. I mean, you cool and all, but I'm trying to find me a husband to take care of me so I can get up out of this apartment."

"Yeah, yeah, yeah," Savannah nonchalantly said as she began removing her clothes.

"Okay, I take it dinner didn't go too well." Tyra walked into the bedroom and plopped across the bed.

"No. Not only did Terrance's nosy aunts treat me like a pariah, but they invited some old homely chick to dinner, trying to hook Terrance up." Savannah pouted as she swept her bushy hair up into a ponytail.

"No, they didn't."

"Yes, they did." Savannah stood before the mirror in her bra and panties, taking in her beautiful chocolate-colored skin and voluptuous figure. Her body could get almost any man she wanted, except the Reverend Terrance Ellis. She'd been going to Lily Grove ever since he took over as pastor, but she didn't take a true interest in getting to know him a little better until a year ago, when she'd jokingly told her grandmother that Terrance was the type of man she needed in her life. Her grandmother had laughed hysterically and told her she had a better chance of "marrying Denzel Washington."

For a while, though, Savannah had thought maybe her grandmother was right, because despite her blatant flirting, Terrance wouldn't give her the time of day until a month ago. She'd almost fallen over backward when he'd asked her out to dinner.

"Are you sure you know what you're doing?" Tyra asked. "I mean, you seem like you're really feeling him. What if he's just, I hate to say this, but what if he's using you as something to do."

Savannah blew a frustrated breath. "I know what I'm doing, okay? I know you and everybody else may find this hard to believe, but Terrance enjoys being with me. I'm just ready to take things to the next level."

Savannah continued to stare at her reflection as she thought about Terrance. He made her feel like somebody. He didn't judge her, and he liked her for who she was. She felt validated around him and had begun having dreams of building a life with him.

"So, you just gonna let his aunts play you like that then?" Tyra asked, snapping Savannah back from her thoughts.

"Please." Savannah pulled open a drawer to search for some lounging clothes. "You know me better than that. Those women got me twisted if they think their nasty attitudes gon' run me off. And the homely chick? No competition."

"They just don't know. What you want, you always get." Tyra laughed.

"You doggone straight. And I want Terrance Ellis." Savannah slipped on a pair of shorts and a tank top.

"I still don't understand that." Tyra shook her head as she turned over on her back. "Why in the world you'd want to be a preacher's wife is beyond me."

"It's not that I just want to be a preacher's wife. I want everything that comes with being Terrance's wife, money, power, respect. Especially respect. Besides, Terrance is a good catch. He's a wonderful man, sweet, fun, and you know how good-looking he is."

"That he is." Tyra did good to make it to church on Christmas and Easter, but when she did go, she spent her entire time there gazing at Terrance. "He looks like Will Smith, only sexier. But still, the fact remains, he's a preacher."

"So? Preachers are men, too. I like Terrance because he's still down. He lets me be me. I mean, couldn't you see me as the first lady?"

"Girl, talk about turning that church upside down." Tyra hesitated. "But this seems like you're trying to be with Terrance because you have something to prove."

Savannah rolled her eyes at her friend. Tyra was only partially right. The most important thing now was that she was really starting to care for Terrance. But she could tell if the hens had their way, she and Terrance would never have a real relationship.

"I just think you're playing with fire," Tyra said, her voice laced with concern. "You're going to end up hurt. Besides, I heard rumors that he was gay."

"Whatever," Savannah tossed out. "Terrance is not gay."

"Yeah, dang near thirty, never married, no documented girlfriends, no baby mamas. Sounds straight to me," Tyra quipped.

"Whatever, Tyra. Just don't hate me when you get the wedding announcement that says introducing Reverend and Mrs. Ellis."

Tyra laughed as she pulled herself up off the bed. "You're delusional. I know his aunts. And they'd just as soon set the church on fire before they let you walk down the aisle with that boy."

"Thanks for the vote of confidence, Tyra." Savannah smiled sarcastically.

"I'm your girl and just keeping it real."

Savannah threw a pillow at the back of Tyra's head as Tyra made her way out of the room. Savannah plopped down on the bed herself. Tyra was right. Getting past Mamie, Eva, and especially Dorothy Mae wasn't going to be easy. But then, nothing in her life had ever been.

chapter 12

"You sure you don't want a beer?"

Terrance cut his eyes at his best friend, Monty Pierce, who was standing over him with two Bud Lights in his hand. "You know better than that."

Monty shrugged before setting one beer on the coffee table, plopping down in his oversize recliner, and popping the top on the other beer. "I keep telling you those people are going to drive you to drink over at that church and it's only a matter of time."

Terrance chuckled. "You may be right about that. But still, alcohol ain't the answer. You don't need to be drinking yourself."

Monty took a long swig of his beer. "God called you to preach, not me." He belched. "Well, actually, He did call me, but then He called back and told me He had the wrong number."

"Boy, you're crazy." Terrance laughed. But his demeanor quickly changed as he let out a long sigh and leaned back on Monty's sofa.

"Dang, man. What's up?" Monty said, eyeing him. "Why are you over here looking all gloomy today? How'd your date with the freak go?"

"Don't call her that." Over the years, Terrance had felt himself growing in a different direction from Monty, and it was things like this—Monty's blatant disrespect for women—that was causing the rift.

"Sorry, Rev, but you know I call 'em like I see 'em."

"Well, I'm getting enough of that from my aunts."

Monty let out another obnoxious belch. "Talk to me, bruh. You always the strong one for everybody else, but even the strong men need someone to vent to from time to time."

"I don't know what to do about Savannah." Terrance sighed, finally deciding Monty was the closest thing to a confidant he was going to get. "I like her, but my aunts are right. There's no way she could ever be a first lady."

"You're right about that. You think those folks are driving you crazy now. Try telling them Savannah is your new woman. I'd have to come to church more often just to get a front-row seat on all the drama." Monty laughed. "Tell me again how you hooked up with her in the first place?" Monty had met Savannah at church a couple of times on the rare occasions that he went. Then they'd all gone out to eat one day last week, but that was the extent of their interaction.

"I guess you can just say she got to me," Terrance replied. "She used to always hang out around the church. I spoke, but never said much else to her, despite her blatant flirting. I don't know, I just never paid her much attention, even when she indirectly asked me out. At first, I kept making excuses. Then I saw her with this young girl she's mentoring, and it was just great watching her in action. And then, I saw everybody just giving her a hard time."

"So, you went out with her because you felt sorry for her?" Monty said, an incredulous look across his face.

Terrance shook his head. "No, I finally decided to go out with her thinking we'd go out once and that would be it. Well, one date turned to two, and before I knew it, we were spending more and more time together."

"I think you were just tired of your dry spell and Savannah is fine, with a capital *F*."

"Naw, that's not it. I mean, I am getting tired of being single. I want to settle down, have some kids, but it's not that easy. I have to find someone I want to be with, and someone that'll make everybody else happy. After hanging out with Savannah, I thought maybe she could be that person, but she can be a little wild, so I just don't know."

"Here's a thought. How 'bout you only worry about making yourself happy?"

Terrance flashed a smile as Monty shook his head. Of course he wouldn't understand. Monty was definitely an it's-all-about-me man. His good looks afforded him his pick of women. And he usually picked top-notch women. After a couple of weeks he would grow bored with them and toss them aside.

"Didn't you say something about your aunts trying to fix you up with someone?" Monty asked.

"Yeah, they called yesterday trying to get me to go out with someone my aunt Eva knows."

"Ooooh, I bet she's a booger bear."

"Actually, I met her before. She was pretty but we didn't talk long."

"You've seen her and she looks all right? Then, shoot, what can a date hurt?"

"I just don't know." Terrance sighed heavily. "I want something real. I'm just not understanding. If there are so many women out there searching for a good man and I'm looking for a good woman, why haven't we found each other?"

"Because your preacher-man status causes the nut-cases to come out and it's hard sifting through them all. But I tell you what." Monty patted Terrance on his back. "As your best friend, I will take it upon myself to help you out. So feel free to send the pretty ones my way, and I'll help you sift through them all in search of Mrs. Right."

Terrance laughed. "Yeah, man. If only it was that easy."

chapter 13

Terrance couldn't believe he was actually out on a date with someone his aunts had fixed him up with.

He had been totally against the idea when his aunt Eva first brought it to him, especially after that disastrous blind date with the girl Monty had fixed him up with. But Eva had looked at him with those sad puppy-dog eyes, which he could never say no to. Then, when she'd told him all about Claire Rollins, and how she was a dedicated nurse, how beautiful and intelligent she was, well, he figured, what was the harm in one date? Maybe if he gave another woman a chance, it could solve the whole dilemma he was having about Savannah.

Claire had turned out to be everything Eva said she was and more. Her almond-shaped eyes dazzled him the minute he walked in the door of Vilini's Italian Restaurant. She had beautiful wavy, shoulder-length hair, the smoothest dark brown skin Terrance had ever seen, and a body that would put Angela Bassett to shame.

Over dinner, they had intelligent, thought-provoking

conversations on everything from music to the state of world affairs. Terrance was beginning to think his aunt had actually done well with this blind date. Then Claire said something that ruined it all.

"I'm sorry. I just don't believe in God."

Terrance wanted to back away from the table for fear that the lightning bolt meant for her would strike him, too.

"Excuse me?" he said, hoping he'd heard her wrong.

"I just think all this God stuff is overrated. I mean, we're putting all our trust in a book written by men."

"But God directed those men to write down His Word," Terrance numbly replied.

"Says who?" Claire nonchalantly retorted. "I mean, none of us were actually there. We just take some quack's word that he was directed by God to come up with this book by which we should all govern our lives. We pass that warped logic down from generation to generation without ever questioning the validity of it." She chuckled. "It's funny, we look at the man who stands on the corner of my neighborhood talking about he's Jesus like he's insane. But if you really think about it, that's exactly what those people who wrote the Bible did. Only we took their word for it."

Terrance was completely speechless. He was expecting that Claire would at any minute burst out laughing like this was some mean-spirited and tasteless joke. But he could tell by the expression on her face that she was dead serious. She looked at him like she was waiting on a valid answer.

"Well, what do you believe in?" Terrance asked, struggling not to sound condescending. His mentor, Dr.

Frank Hilliard, at Arkansas Baptist College, had always taught him to try to reach the nonbelievers. Although, truthfully, he was having a hard time just digesting what she was saying.

"I believe in the tangible, the right here, the right now. I believe in what I can see and touch, and, darling, I can't see or touch your God."

"But you can feel him, right here." Terrance touched his heart.

"Come on, Terrance. I mean, for real, how do we actually know God even exists? Because our ancestors believed it, we have to believe it, too?"

It took Terrance a moment to compose himself. He could not believe he was having this conversation.

"Everything we have, we have because of God's grace," he finally replied.

"That's just it," Claire said with disgust. "How do we know it's God's grace? Why can't it be Venus' grace? Or due to the simple evolution of science? And the whole organized-religion thing, that's just a method of brain-washing people."

Terrance knew he should have gone to the Bible and quoted a number of scriptures, but honestly, he was simply at a loss for words.

"You do know I'm a preacher," he finally managed to say.

She nodded. "But your beliefs don't bother me. If you want to believe in all that foolishness, that's perfectly fine with me."

Good Lord, this woman has lost her mind. Terrance finished his dessert, too stunned to say much else.

"Terrance, I really enjoyed this evening," she said

after eating her last piece of cheesecake. "I hope that we can do this again. Soon." She reached out and gently rubbed his hand.

Terrance quickly pulled his hand back.

"Claire," Terrance began, trying to respectfully form the words that were in his head, "I enjoyed talking to you as well, but this, well, the latter part of our evening has come as quite a shock to me."

Claire looked confused.

Terrance cleared his throat. "I am a man of God, and any woman in my life must be a woman of God, even if she's just a friend."

"Well, that's crazy. Christians can't be friends with non-Christians?"

Terrance pondered her question. "I'm sure they can. But at this point in my life, I'm looking for a Christian woman."

Claire rolled her eyes. "So because I don't believe in God, I don't stand a chance?"

He looked at her pitifully. "No chance at all." He pressed his lips together, then blew a frustrated breath. "Once again, thank you for dinner and have a good evening."

Terrance exhaled as he walked off. He meant it this time, he was absolutely, positively not going on any more blind dates.

"Maybe I just need to stick with Savannah," he mumbled as he climbed into his car. "Because at this point, if I can't find a woman on my own, then I think that means I was just meant to be alone."

chapter 14

Savannah took a deep breath. She knew she should be respectful of other people, especially her elders, but this was too much.

She tried to pretend she didn't see Eva and Mamie standing at the end of the aisle staring her down. Out of all the Wal-Marts in Houston, why they had to be in this one at this time was beyond her.

Savannah debated whether she should put the purple box back on the shelf and just try to walk away. Who was she kidding? They'd seen it clear as day. And her trying to put the box back would only make things worse.

"Umph, hello, Miss McKinney," Eva all but snarled. Even though Savannah had tried to cover up the label on the box clutched tightly in her hand, Eva couldn't help but notice the big Trojan man smiling brightly.

"Planning an eventful night?" Eva asked, her eyes never leaving the box.

Savannah wanted to tell them, so what if she was?

But she was trying to win Terrance's love, and cussing out his aunts was probably not the way to do it.

She cleared her throat. "I'm just picking up a few things," she said, dropping the box down behind her leg. She hated that she had even picked up the stupid box. She just wanted to be prepared in the event she did ever get lucky enough to get Terrance into her bed.

Savannah shifted her weight from one foot to the other. "So, are you ladies coming up with some great ideas for the Christmas celebration?" She wanted to do anything to deflect the uncomfortable silence that hung between them.

"Of course we are," Eva replied matter-of-factly.

"Well, I'd love to serve on a committee, you know, do whatever I can to help." Savannah thought maybe she could win over Terrance's aunts by continually being nice—despite their blatant nastiness.

"Hmmph," Mamie said, rolling her eyes.

"We'll keep that in mind," Eva coldly replied.

Savannah sighed. Maybe her grandmother was right. These people would never accept her. She finally decided to come right out and ask them why they hated her.

"Ms. Eva, no disrespect," Savannah gently said, "but why do you have a problem with me?"

Eva pursed her lips, then looked Savannah in the eyes. "I know your history. And just to be honest with you, that's not what I want for my nephew. I only want what's best for him."

Savannah weighed her words carefully. "How about letting Terrance decide what's best for himself?"

Mamie stepped up. "Look," she began, pointing to

the purple box, "we know your MO. You like to seduce men into getting what you want. And we're not going to stand around and let you do that to Terrance, sleep your way into the first lady's spot."

Savannah fought back the tears, which were building up. "Have you two always been so perfect? And I don't mean that in a sarcastic way. I just want you to think about that. In your world, is it possible that people can change?"

Eva didn't answer, but Mamie turned up her lips like she wasn't trying to hear any argument Savannah might have had. "People can change. We don't believe you can."

Savannah sighed. It was obvious nothing she said would get through to them. Back in the day, she would probably have cursed them out. But she was trying to take a much more mature approach in this relationship with Terrance.

"I'm sorry you feel that way and I truly hope that one day I can change your mind." Savannah set the box back on the shelf and walked away.

chapter 15

"Why is Dorothy Mae not answering this door?" Mamie huffed as she leaned over and peered into Dorothy Mae's living room window. "I know she's in there. I hear all that rumbling."

"I don't know what she's doing, but she needs to come on," Eva added. They'd been standing on Dorothy Mae's porch for almost five minutes, banging on the door. Eva pounded again. "Open the door, Dorothy Mae!"

"I'm coming," Dorothy Mae finally called out.

After another minute, Dorothy Mae cracked open the front door. Her gray hair was all over her head, and she didn't have a drop of makeup on, which was totally out of character for her.

"What took you so long? And why are you still in your robe at five o'clock in the evening?" Eva asked.

"I . . . I just wasn't feeling well, that's all."

"Did you forget we were coming by here today?" Eva asked.

Dorothy Mae squinted. "Oh my goodness. I did forget."

"What's on your mind?" Mamie asked. "We just talked about this yesterday."

"I guess it just slipped my mind and I lost track of time." Dorothy Mae just stood there, staring at them through the screen door.

"Well, you gon' let us in or you gon' make us stand out on this porch?" Mamie said, her irritation becoming evident.

"Oh, yeah, yeah," Dorothy Mae replied, unlatching the screen door, then stepping back to let them in.

Eva and Mamie walked into the living room. Eva was just about to say something when Chester walked out of the kitchen carrying a wrench in one hand and a toolbox in the other.

Both Eva and Mamie looked at Chester, then back at their sister.

"Well, Ms. Dorothy Mae, I got your pipes all cleaned out. Your sink ought to be working fine," Chester nervously said. "Evenin', ladies," he added, nodding toward Eva and Mamie.

"Thank you, Chester," Dorothy Mae mumbled.

"I betta get going now." Chester didn't say another word as he hurried out the door.

As soon as the screen door slammed, Eva and Mamie turned back to Dorothy Mae. The three women just stared at one another.

"What?" Dorothy Mae finally said.

"I bet Chester *did* clean your pipes," Mamie finally cackled. "Got them old things up and running smoothly, I'm sure."

"Mamie, just what are you trying to say?" Dorothy Mae huffed.

"I ain't *trying to say* nothing. I'm straight up telling you, you know your old behind was up here getting your groove on."

Dorothy Mae's mouth dropped open. "How dare you say something like that? Chester was just over helping me."

"Umm-hmm, I'm sure he was," Mamie said. "This the same Chester you act like you can't stand."

Eva finally shook off her surprised look. "Dorothy Mae, if you want to have Chester, ah, clean your pipes, then you go right ahead." She giggled.

"Shoot, I ain't mad at you, chile," Mamie added. "My pipes so clogged, I just done 'bout given up hopes that anything will ever flow between them thangs again."

"Will you two just drop this and tell me what you're doing here," Dorothy Mae demanded as she took a seat in a chair at her dining room table.

Eva quickly filled Dorothy Mae in on their little run-in with Savannah at Wal-Mart.

"So she wants us to give her a chance?" Dorothy Mae mumbled, as Eva finished up the story.

"She sure does," Mamie muttered. "But that little floozy is out of her mind if she thinks that will ever happen."

"But I tell you what," Eva said. "I could tell from the look in her eyes that she was serious. She's going to try to get Terrance any way she can."

Dorothy Mae got up and began pacing the room. "Y'all, this is serious. You know Terrance can't handle a worldly woman like her. She get to seducing him and throwing her womanly wiles on him, it's all over."

"Well, that's why we got to make sure he loses interest in her." Mamie was just about to say something else when Terrance appeared on the other side of the screen door.

"Knock, knock," he said through the door. "Can I come in?"

"Come on, it's open," Dorothy Mae said.

"Hello, everyone." Terrance leaned in and gently kissed each woman. "Aunt Dorothy Mae, you really don't need to be sitting up in here with your doors unlocked. I could've been anyone." He tossed them a suspicious look when no one responded. "Why do I get the feeling you all are plotting something here?"

Eva eyed her sisters, then plastered on a smile. "It's just your imagination, sweetie. What are you doing here? You rushed me off the phone when I called you a little while ago."

"That's because I was on a business call. But since you told me you were coming over here, I just came by to tell you all about my date with Claire."

An excited look crossed Eva's face. She patted the chair next to her. "Oh, yes, have a seat and tell us. How did the date go? Isn't she just wonderful?" Eva was grinning from ear to ear. Her smile quickly faded when she saw the look on Terrance's face.

"No more dates," he said, shaking his head.

"Terrance! Does that mean it didn't go well?" Eva exclaimed like that was definitely not the response she was hoping for.

"Aunt Eva, she's an atheist."

Eva almost fell out of her seat. "What did you say?"

"You heard me. She doesn't believe in God."

Mamie and Dorothy Mae turned to Eva with scowls across their faces.

Eva looked just as shocked. "I didn't know."

"Well, now you do," Terrance replied. "And you know I can't do nothing with a woman who doesn't believe in God."

"But she's a nurse," Eva said, grasping at straws. She'd known Claire's family for over ten years, and no one had ever mentioned Claire didn't believe in God.

"And what does that have to do with anything?" Mamie snapped. "Do you even know anything about this woman? Setting Terrance up with a doggone atheist!"

"Sh . . . she's a nice girl and I know her grandmother, Bettye. And she definitely never said anything about her granddaughter being an atheist," Eva stuttered.

"Probably because she was too ashamed," Dorothy Mae replied.

"Well, whatever the case, I can't do anything with a woman who doesn't believe in God," Terrance repeated as he leaned back in his chair.

"That's why you should've gone out with Rosolyn," Mamie proclaimed.

Terrance cut his eyes. "Who is Rosolyn?" He shook his head. "Wait, never mind, I don't even want to know."

Mamie eased into the seat next to Terrance, a devilish look across her face. "Well, since you asked. She is only that beautiful young woman I invited to dinner, the one you barely talked to because Savannah was pawing all over you. She is as sweet as the day is long, and I think you two would make a perfect couple."

Terrance sighed. "I just said, no more dates." Terrance contemplated reiterating that with more force, then decided he knew the best way to shut their whole matchmaking service down. "Besides, I think Savannah and I are growing closer." He ignored the immediate groans from all three women.

"Terrance, please," Eva pleaded. "She is just . . ."

"Just what? Aren't we all imperfect in some form or fashion?"

"But she takes imperfection to a whole new level," Mamie muttered.

Terrance stood. After that disastrous date with Claire, he'd decided maybe he needed to actually focus on giving Savannah a chance. He was tired of this whole dating scene, and that was definitely to Savannah's benefit.

"Sorry, ladies. This is a done issue. You might as well get to know Savannah because it looks like she'll be sticking around."

Terrance ignored the disgusted looks on his aunts' faces. While he hoped they'd give Savannah a chance, something told him the likelihood of that actually happening was a long shot.

chapter 16

"Okay, you can stop laughing now." Terrance pretended like he was pouting as Raquel doubled over with laughter. They were at her desk, which sat in the massive lobby of his office suite. He hadn't got a chance to talk to her after church yesterday because she'd rushed out as soon as service was over.

"I'm sorry," Raquel said, wiping her eyes. "I'm just envisioning the look on your face as she said she didn't believe in God."

"As you can imagine, it wasn't pretty."

"Well, at least you paid for dinner."

"Don't you have some work to do?" Terrance joked. She was finding this just a little too funny. "Did the save-the-date cards for the Christmas celebration come in?"

Raquel let her laughter die down as she nodded. "They did, although I still don't understand why we're sending them out three months in advance."

Terrance let out a small laugh in defeat. "You pick and choose your battles. The auxiliary committee was adamant about getting the word out early. That was one battle that just wasn't worth fighting, especially with Aunt Eva in charge of publicity."

"I guess you have a point there." Raquel held up a piece of paper. "Well, I have the list and am doing the mail-outs today."

Terrance smiled as he leaned over Raquel's desk and glanced at the paper. "Why did I know you'd be on top of things?" He squeezed her shoulder in a friendly gesture.

Raquel grimaced as she lowered her shoulder. "Ooouch!" She immediately looked like she wished she could take the word back.

Terrance took a step back, his eyes wide. He had barely touched her. "A . . . Are you okay?"

Raquel tried to compose herself. "I'm fine. Just a little sore, that's all." She started trying to busy herself with the papers on her desk. "I've been having these muscle cramps and I really need to go see a doctor. Matter of fact, I think I'll make an appointment today."

Terrance walked around to the front of Raquel's desk. She definitely wasn't a good liar. She couldn't even look him in the eyes.

"Raquel, you know you can always talk to me."

She nodded but still didn't look up. Terrance reached out and put his hands on top of her arms to get her to be still. "Raquel, look at me."

She kept her head down; heaviness seemed to set in her shoulders. That's when he noticed the tears. "What is going on? Did Dolan do something to you?" When she didn't respond, Terrance said, "He did, didn't he."

"No, I'm fine."

"No, you're not. And I can't believe you're sitting here lying to me."

Raquel finally slowly raised her head. "Pastor, I really appreciate your concern. But this is a private matter that I can handle."

"Did he put his hands on you?"

"I can handle this," Raquel said, desperation in her voice.

"I don't care. That doesn't give him the right to put his hands on you, let alone hurt you."

Raquel looked away. "I don't mean to be rude, but I have a lot of work to get done, so if you don't mind . . ."

Terrance stood back. Raquel was pretty, intelligent, definitely not the type of woman he would ever have thought would endure physical abuse. "Fine. If I can't get answers from you, I'll just go ask Dolan."

"No, wait!" Raquel cried, stopping him just as he reached the door. "Please don't do that. It's only going to make things worse."

Terrance slowly turned around. "Then tell me what's going on."

Raquel sighed as she fell back in her chair. "I told you. Dolan gets out of control sometimes. But when he's himself, he's the sweetest man I've ever met."

Terrance walked over and sat down across from her. "I can't believe you're staying with a man who would put his hands on you."

"I couldn't believe it either. At first, I believed his promises that it would never happen again. But then it kept happening again. But don't worry, I'm working on an exit plan. Just one more month and I'll have enough money to get my own place." She sounded like she had thoroughly thought this through. But it wasn't enough for Terrance.

"Yeah, a month. That's plenty of time, if he doesn't kill you first."

That thought didn't seem to come as a shock to her. She hesitated before saying, "Look, Terrance. Please, let me handle this. I'm not a weak woman. I know it may seem like it, but I know what I'm doing, okay? Just trust me."

Terrance just stared at her. No way could he support her in her decision to stay with Dolan, for any amount of time.

"It's my life," she reminded him. "And I'm going to ask you to respect that."

Terrance sighed in defeat. Fine. He'd respect it for now. But he knew deep down, things with Raquel would get a lot worse before they got any better.

chapter 17

Terrance said a silent prayer that he wouldn't see anyone he knew.

"I told you, I'm the bowling champion!" Savannah loudly proclaimed as she pumped her fist in the air. People were starting to stare, but she didn't seem to care. "Get back, get back, you don't know me like that," she sang.

Terrance flashed a forced smile. He couldn't help but notice how the woman next to them outside of Dave & Buster's Entertainment Restaurant kept staring at them. She looked at Terrance and recognition seemed to set in. Then she turned to Savannah and a look of disgust flashed across her face as her eyes roamed up and down Savannah's tight capri pants and black, tight, diamond-studded T-shirt that was cut too low at the top and too high at the bottom.

As much as he enjoyed her company, her attire—and moments like this—had him questioning what he was doing with Savannah.

Terrance was all too relieved when the parking attendant pulled around with his car. He held Savannah's door open while she climbed in his Land Rover.

They had been in the car less than five minutes when Savannah leaned over and whispered in his ear, "Did you enjoy yourself tonight?" She was a lot calmer now. This was the woman he loved being with.

Terrance looked over at her and smiled. He had actually enjoyed himself, until they were leaving and Savannah's loud and boisterous behavior drew stares. "I did have fun," Terrance said, deciding to let his feelings about her behavior go. "I don't think I've been bowling since I was a little kid."

When Savannah had suggested they go do something fun, Terrance had readily agreed. He had been happy for the distraction. He hadn't been able to get his mind off Raquel and her situation with Dolan all day. So he was grateful when Savannah showed up at his office this evening and suggested they go bowling.

Savannah flashed a sexy smirk as she leaned back and gently rubbed the back of Terrance's neck.

"So, am I taking you home now?" Terrance asked as he pulled onto the freeway.

Savannah nodded. "Unless, of course, you have some place else you'd like to go." She had a look in her eyes like she didn't want the night to end.

Terrance headed along Highway 59 toward Savannah's apartment. The way she continued to stroke his neck and back was awakening feelings he had forgotten that he had.

So far, Terrance had been a complete gentleman and hadn't tried anything. But he could tell Savannah was ready for that to change.

"Terrance, can I ask you a question?" Savannah asked, breaking the silence that had filled the truck.

Terrance nodded. "You can ask me anything."

"Where do you see our relationship going?" She paused, like she was unsure if she should continue. "I mean, I've been thinking about it a lot." She took a deep breath. "I really enjoy being with you. And, well, I'd just like to know if you feel the same and where you see us going?"

Terrance didn't know where he saw them going, if there even was a them. One minute he was sure she was the one. The next, he just didn't know. He did know that he enjoyed being with her, but the way she clung to him tonight, and any other time they were out in public, made him extremely uncomfortable. Now he was back to questioning whether they could ever have anything serious.

"Ummm, I like you, too, Savannah. And, umm, I don't know, I guess I hadn't given much thought to a future," he lied. He hated lying, but right about now he simply did not know what to say. Part of him really liked her, but there was something—he couldn't quite put his finger on it—that didn't feel right with her.

Savannah quickly tried to lighten the mood. "Look, let's not even worry about the future right now." She gently ran her fingers along the base of his neck. "Why don't we just worry about the present?"

As if on cue, they pulled in front of her apartment. He parked right in front of her unit, then jumped out to walk around and open her door.

Savannah noticed that he left the truck running, so she reached over, turned it off, and removed the keys, before stepping out of the truck.

"I really would like for you to come inside and tuck me in," she whispered seductively. They were standing so close, he could feel the heat from her breath.

Terrance massaged his neck, then dabbed at the beads of sweat forming on his brow.

"You just don't know . . . ," Terrance said, biting his bottom lip.

Savannah had aroused feelings inside him he hadn't had in ages, since vowing to live his life the right way and wait to have sex with his wife.

"I don't know what?" Savannah asked as she stroked his arm.

"How much I'd love to come inside with you. But me going in there is asking for trouble." Terrance wanted to add that it would be a particularly bad idea since he didn't know where their relationship was headed.

"Come on, T-baby. I'll make it worth your while." She casually ran her tongue across her lips, adding a sparkle to her MAC lip gloss.

"Ummm, Savannah, as enticing as that sounds," Terrance managed to say as he took a step back, "I really need to get going." Terrance knew he had just complained to himself about her outfit, but right now, the skimpy outfit exuded sexiness and a confidence that was completely turning him on.

Savannah playfully stuck out her bottom lip as she took a step toward him. She leaned in to make sure he could get a good view of her hefty cleavage. "Please? I promise you won't be disappointed." For a moment, she looked like she wondered if she was going too far, but when Terrance glanced down, she must have known she was getting to him because she broke out in a big smile.

"I understand you have to uphold a certain standard," she whispered as she ran her finger over his lips. "But it's just me and you tonight. What goes on inside 2934 View Place, stays inside 2934 View Place."

Terrance closed his eyes as he savored her touch. He let out a gentle moan before pulling himself away. "I'm sorry. I'm going to have to pass."

Terrance held out his hand for his keys. Savannah dropped them in his hand, that seductive smile still spread across her face. "I'm not letting up," she purred. "But I will let you go for tonight. I know you want me and it's just a matter of time before you give in to that desire." She kissed him on the lips, sending shivers up his spine, before sashaying up the walkway to her apartment.

She was right. He wanted her. Bad. But he knew sleeping with her would only complicate things. It's bad enough that he was even entertaining the idea of fornicating, but he definitely couldn't do it with Savannah when he knew she wanted a relationship.

Terrance wiped the beads of sweat forming on his forehead as he walked back around and got in the car. He watched as Savannah unlocked her door. She turned, waved, and blew him a sultry kiss. Yes, he needed to hurry up and decide what he was going to do. Because Lord knew it was just a matter of time before the temptation with Savannah became too great.

chapter 18

"So, you just gonna stay in a funk all day?" Tyra said as she stuck her head in Savannah's bedroom. It was after one in the afternoon and Savannah was still in her pajamas. She'd been moping around the apartment all day, and right now she was stretched out across her fuchsia satin queen-size comforter watching paternity tests revealed on the *Maury* show.

"Tyra, I'm not in the mood, okay?" Savannah drily responded. "Besides, Esmeralda is about to test her seventh man to see if he's her baby's daddy."

"It's a rerun and he ain't her baby daddy either. And, no, it's not okay." Tyra walked into the room. She was dressed in her usual sleeveless T-shirt, flowing skirt, and bangled arm. "What's going on with you? And why don't you clean this place up?" she asked, taking in the mounds of clothes strewn across the floor and the empty chips and soda cans that sat on the nightstand.

Savannah let out a long, frustrated sigh as she flipped off the television. "I'm stumped. I pulled out the seduction mode last night and it still didn't work on Terrance."

"Wow. There hadn't been a man yet who passed up your ultimate seduction."

"Who you telling?"

Tyra looked like she was deep in thought. "Well, I guess he is a minister."

"But he's still a man. Right?"

"You're right about that." Tyra sat down on the edge of her friend's bed. "But obviously, this is going to take a little bit more work than we thought."

"Tell me about it. Last night, I was hoping to take things one step further and get him into bed."

"That would have been all she wrote. He would've been trying to get you to run off to Vegas and elope." Tyra laughed. "No, seriously, he just strikes me as the type that's not into casual sex. If he sleeps with you, I think he wants something real."

"I want something real, too. And I know he's feeling me. I can tell. But it's just a part of him that won't let go."

Tyra looked like she was thinking for a moment, then said, "Do you think it's someone else?"

Savannah shook her head. "I don't think so. Terrance is not the type to play games. I think he's just trying to play it safe. Plus, with all those haters at the church, including his aunts, I'm sure it just adds to the pressure of being with me."

"So what are you going to do?"

Savannah threw herself back on her satin pillows. "I don't know. I need to do something. Because time is running out. I have got to get Terrance to see that I'm the woman for him. And, Tyra, I'm going to do whatever it takes to make sure that happens."

"You're really feeling him, huh? I mean, this isn't just some attempt to prove you can get him?"

"I told you, Tyra. This is for real. When I'm with Terrance, it's like I'm no longer that conniving girl from the hood. I feel, I don't know, validated. Like I am somebody."

Tyra stroked Savannah's bushy hair. "Oh, girl, quit trippin'. You are somebody. You don't need no dude to tell you that."

Savannah's eyes watered up. "Do you know what my grandmother said when I called to tell her I was dating Terrance?" Savannah didn't give Tyra time to answer. "She told me to use him for everything I can because ain't no way in hell a man like Reverend Terrance Ellis would want somebody like me."

Tyra bit her lip. "That's messed up."

"That's what everybody says. But it's different hearing it from your own flesh and blood." Savannah let out a long sigh as she struggled to keep the tears at bay. "I want people to see that a woman like me can get a good man like that. And not to mention that I really do like him."

Savannah thought back to her last serious boyfriend. They'd dated for six months and Savannah thought he was really the one. She found out he wasn't on the day of his wedding.

When Savannah had asked him how he could do that to her, what about their future, he'd replied curtly, "Come on, baby girl, you can't really think I ever wanted anything serious with you."

She never let on, but that had torn at her soul. Sure, she'd used men in the past, but she wanted something different now. She wanted a nice, quiet, stable life with a man she didn't have to worry about breaking her heart. Terrance could provide that life. That was her dream, and Savannah was prepared to do whatever it took to ensure that her dream came true.

chapter 19

Terrance had just pulled out of the church parking lot when he noticed the tall, fair-skinned woman leaning against her car, frustration on her face. She had the hood up and looked like she had no idea what to do.

Naturally, he pulled up in front of her, got out, then walked back to her car.

"Hi there. Seems like you're having a little car trouble."

The woman exhaled as she ran her fingers through her jet-black hair. "Try a lot of trouble. This dang thing just up and quit."

Terrance leaned over and looked under the hood, not that he had any idea what he was looking at. He definitely was not mechanically inclined.

"Have you called a tow truck?"

"I have. My brother actually. He works for a towing company. He'll be here, but not for another two hours. He's on a job." She pulled her pink wrap around her body. "It's cool out here, I'm tired, and I just hate that

I have to stay out here and wait. I can't even start the dumb thing to push it off to the side."

Terrance looked around, wondering if he should open the church back up and let her wait in there. He glanced at his watch. He was supposed to be meeting Deacon Tisdale to pick up some papers at Starbucks near the Galleria, which was about fifteen minutes away. "Well, I know you don't know me from Adam, but I'm Terrance Ellis, the pastor of Lily Grove," he said, pointing back to the church.

"Oh, I've heard of you. Never had the chance to visit your church, but I've heard great things about it." The woman finally smiled, revealing a set of beautifully white and perfectly straight teeth.

"Well, you should come to visit one Sunday. We would love to have you." Terrance paused and looked at his watch again. "But, look, why don't you ride with me to Starbucks? I have to pick up some papers from someone there. We can have a cup of coffee, then I can bring you back. That ought to kill about two hours."

She looked around nervously. "You know, that sounds like a great idea."

"Let me just lower your hood while you lock up your car. It should be fine here until we get back." Terrance walked over and pushed the hood down while she grabbed her purse and locked the doors.

"So, I didn't get your name," Terrance said once they were in the car and heading toward the freeway.

"I'm sorry, where are my manners? It's Debra. Debra Wright." She grinned slyly.

*   *   *

After Terrance had signed the papers Deacon Tisdale needed, he settled at a corner table with Debra, who had ordered them both two small cups of coffee.

"I hope plain coffee is fine?" she said.

"It is. In this era of peppermint, mocha, vanilla crème, it's probably a rarity, but it's still my preference nonetheless." He flashed a smile as he took a sip of the coffee. "Although you should've let me pay for it."

"Nonsense. It's the least I can do. You're a lifesaver," she said, fingering her cup.

"So, Mrs. Wright, do you live by the church?"

"It's Debra, please. And just so you know, it's Miss, not Mrs. And, no, I was just visiting a friend in that neighborhood. I actually live in Sunnyside."

Terrance's eyebrows shot up. "You don't say?" Sunnyside was a rough area and she seemed anything but rough.

"The neighborhood is not as bad as people like to make it out to be. I actually grew up there and it's a nice neighborhood, full of hardworking families."

"Oh, I don't doubt that," Terrance said. "You just seem, a little, I don't know, refined."

"Oh, so classy women can't come from rough neighborhoods?" She shot him a look like she was offended. For a minute he thought she was serious, but then she broke out in a huge smile. Her smile was contagious.

Terrance covered his face with his hand. "I'm sorry, I didn't mean that like it sounded. Let me get my foot out of my mouth and start again."

She smiled and lightly touched his hand. "Don't worry about it. I'm just giving you a hard time."

They exchanged pleasantries for another ten minutes

before she began sharing personal details with him. He was a little surprised at her candidness. She had openly told him that she was twenty-six, single, and hoped to one day get married and have children. She said she worked for a bank in downtown Houston and took real estate classes at night so she didn't get out much and meet people.

Terrance was amazed at how well they had clicked, and before he knew it, two hours had passed. "Oh, wow," he said when he noticed the time, "we'd better get you back or you'll miss your brother."

Terrance and Debra continued their conversation as they made their way back to the church. His heart warmed when she began talking about her relationship with God. Despite not having achieved everything she wanted in life, she continuously talked about how blessed she was.

They had just turned onto the street to the church when her mouth dropped open. "Oh my God. My car is gone!"

Terrance peered down the empty street. "It is gone."

"Do you think someone had it towed? Or worse, stole it?"

"If it was broken-down, a thief probably wouldn't have been able to get it so quickly. And no one calls tow trucks around here. Maybe your brother came early." Terrance came to a stop in the place they'd left her car.

"But he would've at least called." Debra looked at her phone. "Oh, no, four missed calls. I must've not heard the phone ringing in the coffee shop."

She flipped the pink Razr open and punched in a few numbers to call her voice mail. After listening to her messages, she let out a groan as she pushed the end button and snapped the phone closed.

"Just great," she moaned. "My brother came and got the car. He towed it to the repair shop. He said since I wasn't here, he just assumed I found a ride home. So now what am I gonna do?"

"Well, the good thing is, it's been a while since I've been to Sunnyside and I was just thinking I needed to get back to cruise the neighborhood. So what better time than now?" he joked.

"Oh, yeah, visiting Sunnyside is right at the top of the tourist attractions in the city of Houston brochure," she replied, her cute dimples singing to him. "But since you're headed that way, I would be more than happy to ride along." Her expression turned serious. "Terrance, you have been a lifesaver all the way around today."

Debra gave him the directions to her house. They chatted some more as they made the twenty-minute drive to her neighborhood. As Terrance pulled up in front of Debra's house, she squeezed his hand. "Thank you so much for being a gentleman. In this day and age, a lot of men wouldn't have done that, and I really appreciate it."

"Don't worry about it."

"No, you'll have to let me repay you. Let me cook you dinner or something. I'm a heck of a cook. You haven't tasted anything until you've tasted my smothered pork chops and onions."

"Ummmm, that sounds delicious, and I just might have to take you up on that offer." An image of Savannah quickly flashed through Terrance's mind. He felt a twinge of guilt because he knew she wouldn't approve of his being out with another woman—even if they didn't have a commitment. If Savannah wasn't the one, here was an opportunity to see if maybe Debra was.

Terrance grabbed his business card from the console, wrote down his personal phone number, and handed it to her. "Give me a call."

She smiled. "It sounds great. I can't wait."

Terrance couldn't help but grin as he drove off. He had a really good feeling about Debra. Finally, he felt like he'd found a woman who might really be a prospect.

chapter 20

Eva tried her best to plaster on a smile. Honestly, she didn't feel like smiling at the men who were trying to ease her nephew out of his job just because he didn't have a woman.

But they were standing there, grinning like they'd won the Lotto or something.

"Well, hello, Sister Eva," Deacon Tisdale said as she walked by. Eva wanted to tell him to take his old decrepit self to the dentist and get a set of dentures.

"Hello, Brother Tisdale." Eva took her seat at the conference table. She wished Mamie and Dorothy Mae would hurry up and get there. She hated being alone with these men that she couldn't stand.

Honestly, their relationship had been all right until that day she overheard them talking about Terrance. Ever since then, she hadn't really had two words to say to them.

"Your lovely sisters on their way?" Deacon Tisdale said.

"They'll be here in a minute." Eva tried to flash a smile.

"Well, I reckon we can go ahead and get started," Deacon Tisdale announced. "I am happy to say that plans are moving full speed ahead for the Christmas service. We got commitments from four more churches this week."

"And Reverend Wilkerson over at New Jeremiah said his wife would be more than willing to host the First Ladies' Brunch," Louis tossed in, as he casually looked toward Eva. "You know, since we ain't got nobody to host it here."

Eva bit down on her lip. "That won't be necessary. My sisters and I have decided we'll host it again." They hadn't, but Eva knew Mamie and Dorothy Mae would be up for the idea, which had just come to her, even though they'd vowed last year was their last time doing it.

"No disrespect, Sister Eva, but this is a tradition that dates back seventy-five years with this church. How we gon' have a First Ladies' Brunch, hosted by someone who isn't a first lady?"

Eva fanned herself with her handkerchief. It was sixty degrees outside but she definitely felt warm in here, maybe because they had her blood pressure on the rise. "I don't see what the big deal is."

"You wouldn't," Carl mumbled, "since it's your nephew that's causing this whole dilemma."

Eva threw her handkerchief down. "So what would you suggest, Brother Baker? Terrance—I mean, Reverend Ellis—should just go pick up some ninny off the street and marry her so that we'll have someone to host a stupid breakfast?" Eva had tried to keep her composure, but they were making it difficult.

"All I'm saying is there's all kinds of respectable women in this church—shoot, in this town. The reverend ought to be able to find somebody that's suitable enough to be his wife. That is, unless he's . . ."

"Unless he's what, Carl? Say it. Say it so I can slap the taste outta your mouth," Eva threatened.

Deacon Tisdale held up his hands. "Now, now. No need to get all worked up. I think Brother Baker has a valid concern. We're all concerned. Even if you ladies did host the event again, it's bound to raise eyebrows and have people asking similar questions, whether we like it or not."

"It just don't make no sense for the boy to be dang near thirty and not even have a girlfriend." Carl leaned forward, ignoring the chastising look of Deacon Tisdale. "I'm tired of us tiptoeing around like this ain't an issue for everybody. I ain't the only one that thinks like this. And when hundreds of folks pile into this church for the Christmas service, they gon' wonder, too. So, I gots to ask. If the boy don't want a woman, we need to know, right here and now, do he want a man?" Carl glared at Eva.

Eva was just about to give Carl a few choice words that would surely not be pleasing in the eyes of the Lord. But the sound of the door opening stopped her. Terrance was standing there, Mamie and Dorothy Mae by his side.

"Gentlemen, let me answer that," Terrance said, as he walked in the room and took a seat at the head of the conference table. He'd actually been standing at the door for a minute listening to their conversation and had only come in because his aunts walked up. "First of all, my apologies for running late. I had to deal with some church business. Secondly,"—he turned to Carl—"I have no interest in a man. None whatsoever."

Carl leaned back and turned up his lips like he wasn't convinced at all.

Terrance pulled out his organizer and opened it up. "Personally, I'm offended that my personal life has begun to overshadow the true mission of what this Christmas celebration is all about. We are coming up on the time of year when we should be rejoicing in the birth of our Lord and Savior. This celebration is about that, and recognizing one hundred years of service Lily Grove has provided the community and our members. I don't think it should matter whether I have a girlfriend or wife, or whether I'm all by myself."

"Well, Pastor, as noble as that sounds, we're just dealing with the reality," Carl sarcastically responded.

Terrance let out a sigh. He didn't really understand what the big deal was. But as the church's leader, he knew he would have to address it at some point. Today, however, would not be the day. He simply was not in the mood. He had a lot weighing on his mind. That good feeling he'd been having with Debra was starting to wear off. And it had been less than a week since they'd met. She'd called his phone thirteen times yesterday because she had been unable to get in touch with him.

His mind went back to the real reason he'd been late to the meeting, his telephone conversation with Debra.

"Where have you been?" she had screamed at him when he answered the office phone. "I've been calling your cell phone all day!"

"Excuse me?" Terrance had replied.

"Tell me the truth, you're seeing someone else. That's it, isn't it?"

Terrance had quickly blown her off, telling her he had to get to a meeting. She'd gone off for five more minutes before he'd finally just hung up the phone.

"So what do you think, Pastor?"

"Huh?" Terrance said, snapping out of his thoughts. He couldn't believe he'd become so unfocused.

"I think it's the craziest idea I ever heard," Mamie said. She and Dorothy Mae had taken seats next to Eva.

"What are you all talking about?" Terrance asked, looking across the room.

"Have you not listened to anything this moron said in the last five minutes?" Mamie barked.

Deacon Tisdale raised his hand. "Now, now, Sister Russell, there's no need for name-calling."

Mamie didn't reply as she just rolled her eyes. Eva stepped in and said, "Terrance, Brother Baker here wants us to hire an actress to play the role of your fiancée at the church celebration."

Terrance's mouth dropped open. "You're kidding me, right?"

"All I'm saying is that way we won't have folks wagging their tongues about us."

"I don't care about anyone wagging their tongue," Terrance admonished. "I am not about to hire someone to deceive this church or our visitors."

Carl shrugged. "Suit yourself, then. We'll just let our

celebration be marred by the fact that you don't have a woman."

"Where's your woman, Carl?" Mamie snapped.

"I gots me plenty of women," Carl responded.

"That ain't nothing to be proud of," Dorothy Mae interjected.

"Now, now," Deacon Tisdale said, trying to regain control of the meeting. "Pastor is right. We are not here to discuss his love life. If he chooses not to have a woman represent the church by the Christmas celebration, then so be it. We'll deal with the consequences and repercussions."

Terrance cut his eyes. They were talking like he was committing a cardinal sin by not being in a serious relationship.

"You know what, Deacon Tisdale, you can make it sound as vile as you like. The bottom line is that this is a planning meeting for the Christmas celebration. That's all I want to talk about, nothing else. Do all of you understand me?"

Most of the people in the room mumbled, "Yes." Eva smiled proudly.

Another committee member then gave a status report on the guest speaker for the brunch, Rachel Adams from Zion Hill. Eva immediately began spouting reasons why she didn't want Rachel, with her "storied history," to be a featured speaker at the brunch.

Terrance had to silently say a quick prayer. Not only did he need the strength to keep dealing with these people, but right about now he found himself wishing the meeting would hurry up and end because he'd rather be any place than in this church.

chapter 21

"You see, that's exactly what I'm talking about, Terrance. It's like they're obsessed with finding you a woman," Mamie muttered as she walked down the long hallway behind Terrance.

Terrance fought back a groan. It was bad enough he'd spent two hours meeting with the deacons and the rest of the Christmas committee, but now he had to continue to hear about it as his aunts followed him back into his office.

"If you would just give Rosolyn a chance, I think all of your problems would be solved," Mamie tried to reason.

Terrance glared at his aunt. "It doesn't look like the deacons are the only ones obsessed with finding me a woman."

Mamie was just about to protest when Raquel stuck her head in his office.

"Pastor, don't forget about your seven-o'clock meeting. You don't want to keep them waiting."

For a minute, Terrance looked confused. Then he said,

"Right, right. Thank you for reminding me, Raquel." He quickly started gathering up his things. "Ladies, I don't mean to rush you, but I've got to get these papers ready for my meeting."

Eva sighed. "Fine. We'll finish this discussion Sunday over dinner."

Right about now, Terrance had no desire to come over for dinner. But he knew the sooner he agreed, the sooner they'd leave. "Fine, see you Sunday."

Terrance met Raquel in the hall. "Have I told you you're the greatest?" he leaned in and whispered.

"Not today you haven't." She smiled. "I hate lying to your aunts, but I knew you wanted to get out of there. I could see it all over your face."

"You know me so well." He chuckled. "It's been such a long day and I just want to go home and rest. All this woman talk is driving me crazy."

"Well, the sooner you find you one, the sooner they'll leave you alone."

"Don't you start, too," he groaned.

"You know I'm just messing with you. They're trying to use this Christmas celebration as a reason to get you a woman. You don't do anything until you're ready," Raquel warned.

"I'm glad you see things my way."

"Of course." She leaned in and adjusted his tie. "Now, you go on home, get you some rest, and—"

"Awwwwww, so is this why you kept blowing me off!"

Both Terrance and Raquel turned toward the loud screaming coming down the hallway. Terrance looked on in shock as the bellowing woman came at him like a raging bull.

She stopped right in front of him, a look across her face like she wanted to claw his eyes out. "You know I thought we connected, but you just like all the rest of them trifling, no-good men I've dealt with." She spun on Raquel, who stood with a look of horror on her face. "And who is this trick?"

Terrance tried to shake off his shock. "Excuse me, Debra, but I'm going to have to ask you to lower your voice."

"I ain't lowerin' jack. You think you can just play with people's emotions. Lead me on, then just not call me and try to blow me off."

Terrance stared at her. She had to truly be insane. "Debra, I'm sorry if you got the wrong impression."

"Excuse me," Raquel interrupted. "Maybe I'd better leave you two alone."

Debra snarled at Raquel, "Maybe you'd better."

"No, Raquel, you don't have to go anywhere. Miss Wright here was just leaving."

Debra folded her arms across her chest and wiggled her neck. "I ain't leaving nowhere." It's like she was a different person from the woman he'd initially met.

"Maybe you should take this out of the hallway," Raquel said, looking nervously around.

"Nah, we can do this right here," Debra announced, her voice getting louder. "Because everybody needs to know their pastor is a *d, o,* double *g!*"

"What in God's name is going on out here?" Eva asked as she made her way into the hall.

"Debra?" Dorothy Mae said, peering at her friend's daughter.

"Hey, Mrs. Dorothy Mae," Debra said, her voice still laced with attitude. "I'm here to give your jackleg nephew a piece of my mind, let him know he's not gon' play with my emotions and just toss me aside." She raised her voice at a still-stunned Terrance.

"You got me messed up," Debra continued, wiggling her neck. "I don't care what kind of big shot you are around here, that doesn't give you the right to play with people's feelings."

Eva gasped. "Good Lord."

"Debra," Terrance said, seeming to finally come out of his shock, "I don't know what you think I did to lead you on. We had a cup of coffee and a few conversations. That's it. Nothing more."

"That's it?" she barked. "We bonded. We talked on the phone about stuff I've never talked to another man about. You prayed for me and everything, and you talking about that's it?"

"I pray for everybody," Terrance calmly responded.

"You told me you were ready to settle down as soon as you found Mrs. Right," she whined. "Well, I'm Miss Wright, and I'm your Mrs. Right! If that ain't divine, I don't know what is!" Debra was shaking, she was so worked up.

Dorothy Mae stepped up and gently placed her hand on Debra's arm. "Baby, did you take your medication today?"

Both Eva and Mamie snapped their heads toward Dorothy Mae and said in unison, "Medication?"

Terrance looked at Dorothy Mae, confusion etched across his face. "How do you know Debra?"

Dorothy Mae ignored him and tried to stroke Debra's back. "Sweetie, did you take your medication today?" she calmly repeated.

"I told Mama I ain't taking that mess no more. It makes me drowsy and I don't wanna be drowsy!" Debra exclaimed. "I need all my senses so I can sniff out dogs like Terrance." She spun back toward Terrance, her eyes red with rage. "Besides, I thought I'd found me a man and I wouldn't need those stupid pills anymore."

Dorothy Mae gently guided Debra toward the back conference room. "Come with me, sugar. Let's call your mama, then you can tell me all about how my nephew dogged you out."

That seemed to pacify Debra because she sniffed, rolled her eyes at Terrance, then followed Dorothy Mae to the back.

Fifteen minutes later, Dorothy Mae walked into Terrance's office, where everyone had gathered. All eyes were on her as soon as she entered the room.

"We're listening," Eva said as she crossed her arms. "I just know you did not try to fix Terrance up with a crazy woman. And I told you that little plan to pretend Debra's car had broken down was going to backfire."

Dorothy Mae looked apologetic. "I'm sorry."

"You fixed Terrance up with some cuckoo bird?" Mamie asked, astonished.

Dorothy Mae plopped down in a chair. "She's not cuckoo. She has bipolar disorder."

"Like I said, cuckoo," Mamie snapped.

"Her mother said she's fine as long as she takes her medication. And besides, every time I've ever seen her, she's been the perfect sweetheart."

"Did that raving lunatic look like a sweetheart to you?" Eva questioned. "I mean, good Lord, this doesn't make any sense."

"Yeah, Dorothy Mae. How you gon' fix Terrance up with somebody like that?" Mamie chimed in.

"Oh, like the atheist was that much better," Dorothy Mae retorted.

"Okay, that's enough." Terrance rubbed his head. He had a pounding headache.

Dorothy Mae diverted her eyes in shame.

"I can't believe this was a setup." He slammed his hands on his desk. "I want you all to listen up and listen up good. First of all, there will be no more blind dates. No carefully orchestrated meetings. Nothing. Understood?"

"But—," Eva began.

"But nothing. No more dates, no more setups, no more accidental meetings. Nothing. Period. Do you understand that?" Terrance knew he'd caught them off guard with the firmness in his voice, but this was getting out of control. "I will find my own woman. And if I don't find her, then it was not meant for me to have one. Do you understand that?"

"Fine," all three of them muttered.

"Secondly," Terrance continued, "I'm going home. By myself, and please, unless someone dies, nobody call me until tomorrow."

Terrance stomped out of the church determined more than ever to end his search for the perfect wife. After all he'd been through, his future wife was going to have to find him, because he was done searching for the real Mrs. Right.

chapter 22

"So is Terrance still mad at us?" Dorothy Mae asked as she put away the last of the dishes in Eva's kitchen. This was the second Sunday Terrance had skipped out on their weekly meal. This time he didn't even bother to try to give them an excuse. He just didn't show up.

"Your guess is as good as mine." Eva sighed. It looked like their plan to find Terrance a wife was falling apart at the seams.

"Well, last Sunday, I heard he was at Red Lobster having dinner with Savannah." Mamie said Savannah's name like it was an infectious disease.

"I wonder if he's with her again today," Eva said.

Dorothy Mae suddenly got an uneasy look on her face. "Well, I . . . ummm, I found out some information that we might be able to use to nip that relationship in the bud."

Both Eva and Mamie spun around. "What? And you're just now telling us about this?"

Dorothy Mae sat down, suddenly getting excited.

"A little birdie might have told me that Miss Savannah McKinney might actually be a Mrs."

"What?" Eva exclaimed.

Dorothy Mae reached over in her purse and pulled out a piece of paper. "I had a little background check done on Savannah, and as it turns out she married some hoodlum in 1999 and never got divorced."

"So you mean she's married?" Eva asked.

Dorothy Mae laid the marriage license on the table. "Yep. Her husband is in the pen for armed robbery. Shoot, they probably running a scheme trying to take Terrance for his money."

All three women broke out in huge grins. "A little detail I'm very sure she forgot to tell Terrance," Mamie said as she picked up the marriage license and scanned it.

"Then it looks like we'll have to be the ones to break the news," Eva announced.

"And if this doesn't get rid of Miss Thang, I don't know what will," Dorothy Mae added, finally feeling like they had Savannah beat. "And after we're done with her, we'll just see who's showing who."

Mamie scurried into the kitchen. "Are you ready to do this?" she asked her sisters.

"Ready as ever," Eva proclaimed. It had taken a lot of coaxing to convince Terrance to come by. He especially thought they were up to something when Eva invited Savannah. But he'd finally agreed. They'd arrived over an hour ago, and it had been excruciating trying to make it through dinner without saying anything. Dinner had been pure torture. Savannah would smirk at them, then plaster on an innocent look whenever Terrance looked her way. She dabbed at his mouth and fawned over him like he was Jesus himself. The whole thing was sickening. Dorothy Mae had wanted to reveal Savannah's scam the minute she walked in the door, but Eva had convinced her that they needed to tread lightly.

But now was the time. They had wrapped up dessert and Terrance had leaned back in his chair, stuffed. He had his arm around the back of Savannah's chair and she was eating it up.

Eva, Dorothy Mae, and Mamie walked back in and stood over the dining room table.

"Mrs. Lewis, thank you so much for that awesome meal. I wish that I could cook like that," Savannah purred. "Specially since I see how much T-baby loves your cooking."

Eva didn't respond as she struggled to keep a scowl from her face.

Dorothy Mae began blurting out, "Terrance, we have something we'd like—"

Eva held up her hand, cutting Dorothy Mae off. "We just wanted to talk to you guys a little bit, that's all," Eva said as she sat down. "Mamie, Dorothy Mae, sit down." Eva shot them a glare to let them know she had things under control. They shot her a look back to let her know they were tired of waiting.

"Well, Savannah, it looks like things are getting a little serious between you and my nephew," Eva said.

Savannah squeezed Terrance's hand. "I hope so." She smiled lovingly at him.

Eva had to fight back the bile building in her stomach.

"So, is he someone you could see yourself building a future with?"

Terrance suddenly became uneasy and sat up. "Aunt Eva!"

"I'm just asking the girl," Eva calmly responded. "You wanted us to get to know one another."

"No, it's no problem," Savannah replied, thinking to herself, *Are they actually finally coming around to give me a chance?* "Terrance is definitely the type of man I could see myself spending the rest of my life with."

"Yeah, because Terrance ain't never robbed nobody," Dorothy Mae spat.

Terrance shot his aunt a confused look.

"Excuse me?" Savannah said.

"Nothing," Dorothy Mae replied, looking at Eva like she wished she'd hurry up with her line of questioning.

"I think what my sister is saying is that Terrance is a good man," Eva continued.

"I know that." Savannah was starting to get suspicious. Something just didn't feel right.

"Then why are you trying to run games on him?" Mamie snapped, finally jumping into the conversation.

"Aunt Mamie, what in the world are you talking about?" Terrance asked.

Eva leaned back, giving Mamie the go-ahead to spill the beans.

"Did your little Pop-Tart here mention that she was married?" Mamie barked.

Terrance moved his hand from Savannah's grasp. "What?"

"Yep, been married eight years to some thug in prison who's doing time for armed robbery," Mamie announced, as she, Eva, and Dorothy Mae all glared at Savannah.

Savannah, however, didn't seem fazed as a small smile crossed her face. "So it seems you've been doing some digging?" Savannah said, finally figuring out their game.

"We sure have, you lying floozy," Dorothy Mae said.

Terrance looked at Savannah. "What are they talking about? Are you married? To somebody in prison?"

Savannah kept her eyes glued to the three women. "If your nosy aunts had kept digging, they would have seen that I never married anyone. My janky cousin, who had warrants for her arrest and didn't want to risk going to jail, stole my birth certificate and driver's license and got a marriage license in my name so that she could marry her convict boyfriend."

Mamie threw up her hands. "Oh, come on. You can't come up with a better lie than that?"

Savannah shrugged. "It's not a lie," she replied nonchalantly. "If you'd had dug a little deeper, you would have seen that not only did I file a police report, but the marriage under my name was reversed." She turned to Terrance. "I have the paperwork at home and it's a matter of public record."

Eva, Mamie, and Dorothy Mae looked like they didn't know what to believe. Neither did Terrance, who was rubbing his head.

Savannah scooted back from the table, a victorious look across her face. She wanted to straight curse these women out, but for once, she had the upper hand. Everything she'd said had been the God's honest truth, and when she proved it to Terrance, it would bolster her credibility to a whole other level. No sense in ruining it by going off on his aunts.

"Ladies, I'm sorry that you feel like you had to resort

to digging in my past to try and find a reason to keep me from your nephew," Savannah said as she stood up. "I care for him, I really do. And I'm sorry that that's not enough for you."

Savannah walked into the living room and grabbed her purse. She turned toward Terrance.

Eva sat stunned, not really sure what to say. She glared at Savannah. Was that heifer about to cry?

"Terrance, I'm truly hurt," Savannah said, her voice cracking. "But it doesn't change how I feel about you. Could you please take me home? I'll show you the paperwork, which thankfully I've kept, and we can even call my cousin if you'd like. I pressed charges and she got probation for forgery so she can tell you everything I said is true. After that, I hope that you'll understand I have no secrets from you."

Terrance turned to his aunts. He wasn't quite sure what to believe. But if Savannah was indeed telling the truth, he'd be hard-pressed to forgive his aunts for this one.

"I can't believe you guys sunk this low," Terrance muttered as he got up and followed Savannah out the door.

chapter 23

Beat it. Please. I'm bringing him home.

Savannah had quickly texted that message to Tyra while Terrance stepped out to gas up his truck.

They had ridden much of the way in silence, with Terrance simply offering up a meek apology for his aunt's actions.

"I understand. You're their baby," Savannah had replied, rubbing his arm. Inside, she was turning backflips. This couldn't have turned out better if she'd planned it herself. As soon as she got home, she planned to show him the police report, the marriage annulment, and the affidavit her cousin had signed so that Savannah wouldn't be held accountable for anything that fool Rico, the man her cousin had married, might do. Yep, after Terrance saw all that, it was on. Their fate would be sealed. He would be so angry with his aunts, and so pleased with the dignified way that she'd handled herself, that he would have to give their relationship a serious chance.

Twenty minutes later as he pulled in front of her apartment, Savannah turned to Terrance. "I know you're always in a hurry. But please come inside so I can show you the papers. I don't want there to be any doubt, and I don't want anyone to be able to say I had time to doctor up or create some papers."

Terrance ran his hand over the back of his head. He didn't need this drama in his life.

"Please, for me. It would crush my heart if you thought that I had been lying to you."

Terrance forced a smile, then cut off the engine. He quietly followed her up the walkway to her apartment.

Savannah inhaled thankfully when she didn't see Tyra's car. "I hope my roommate didn't leave the apartment a mess. If she did, you'll have to excuse it. Even though it's kinda small, it can be hard to keep clean."

Terrance just grunted. He wanted to tell her the cleanliness of her place was the last thing he was interested in.

Inside, Savannah set her purse down and went straight to her bedroom. Terrance followed her and watched as she pulled a box off the top shelf in her closet. All kinds of emotions were running through his head.

"Here." Savannah handed him the box. "It should be at the top of the stack of papers."

"You don't have to do this."

"I want to. I want you to trust me."

Terrance slowly took the box and sat down on the bed.

"I'm going to go get a glass of wine. Would you like anything?"

He shook his head and slowly lifted the top of the box.

Savannah couldn't help but smile as she headed toward the kitchen.

Terrance took a deep breath as he began perusing the papers. He felt both relief and disgust as he read the police report and subsequent affidavit. Everything Savannah had said was true, which meant his aunts had crossed the line. This was the last straw. They'd gone too far, and he couldn't blame Savannah if she never forgave them.

Terrance eased the papers back in the box, placed the box back on her closet shelf, and made his way into the living room. Savannah was seated on the leather sofa, her legs crossed, slowly bobbing her head to the light jazz that was filling the room. She had a glass of wine in her hand and seemed lost in thought.

Terrance spent a moment watching her. She really was beautiful. Maybe she was a little rough around the edges because it was all she'd ever known. Maybe, with a little refining, she could really be a first lady the church would accept.

He inhaled and walked over to the sofa. She lightly smiled as he sat down next to her.

"I don't even know how to begin telling you how sorry I am," he said, his voice soft and low.

"Don't worry about it. Your aunts are just concerned about you, that's all. They want to make sure you're getting with the right woman."

"But they were so out of order."

"Sssshh." She reached over and handed him a glass of wine.

Normally, Terrance wasn't much of a drinker, but after the day he'd had, he needed something to ease his nerves.

He took the wine, sipped it, and leaned back. "I'm sorry, Savannah. I just don't know what to do about my aunts. I love them, but they are getting totally out of hand."

Savannah couldn't believe her luck. Terrance was exactly where she wanted him. She gently caressed the back of his neck as he continued to vent. He spent the next ten minutes going on about how his aunts had run his life for as long as he could remember.

"It's been this way my whole life and I'm tired of it. They run off anyone I'm remotely interested in, and I think I just got to the point where I stopped even trying. I just immersed myself in my work, and soon dating didn't become as important to me." He sighed.

"I know your work is important, but while you're taking care of everything and everyone else, it might be nice to have someone take care of you," she softly said.

Terrance turned to her and smiled. Savannah could tell the wine was getting to him. His glass was empty again. She'd already filled it twice. She wanted to refill it again, but she didn't want to break the moment.

She took her chances and gently laid her head on his shoulder.

"Thank you for listening."

"That's what I'm here for, baby." She slowly looked up and kissed his cheek. She waited a moment to gauge his reaction. When he closed his eyes, she kissed him again, this time on the lips. It was a simple kiss at first, but when she felt his shoulders relaxing, she added intensity and allowed her tongue to flicker along his lips.

Terrance moaned, a part of his brain telling him he needed to stop before he crossed a line he wasn't sure he was ready to cross. But it had been so long since he'd felt a woman's touch. He had really been trying to live a godly lifestyle, but it had been difficult. And sitting here with Savannah now kissing his neck wasn't making things any better.

"Terrance, don't you want me?" Savannah whispered.

Terrance finally opened his eyes. He stared at her. Both she and Monty were right, he had to start making himself happy. And right about now, nothing would make him happier than making love to her.

"Yes, Savannah, I want you so bad," he moaned.

Without another word, she stood and guided him back to her bedroom. Terrance followed, his mind in a daze. As she slowly undressed, he couldn't help but mutter, "God forgive me," before taking his clothes off as well.

chapter 24

Terrance had never been more confused. As good as making love to Savannah had been, he'd felt extremely guilty afterward and vowed that it would not happen again. But since he'd been hanging with Savannah regularly for the past three weeks, that was proving difficult. He had prayed and fasted in an effort to stay strong. He'd also asked that she respect his decision to abstain from sex. Still, it was hard.

"But I don't understand what's so wrong with two people who are obviously feeling each other to share themselves in such an intimate way," she'd said one night as they sat in his townhome watching movies.

That night, she was clad in a miniskirt that left little to the imagination and a low-cut, tight blouse.

Terrance shifted, trying to ease his uncomfortableness. "Savannah, it's just that I can't, as a man of God, get up every Sunday morning and preach one thing and live my life a totally different way. It would be hypocritical."

Savannah rolled her eyes. "Oh, come on, T-baby. It's not like pastors don't have sex. Shoot, half of them are no good anyway."

"I think that's a slight exaggeration. But the bottom line is, all I care about is this pastor." He pointed to his chest. "And I want to live a godly life."

He could tell she didn't agree, but she'd stopped pouting and ceased trying to get him into bed at every turn. Now, they'd settled into a comfortable routine. And while he did enjoy spending time with her, she still didn't feel like "the one."

"Knock, knock," Raquel said, peeking her head in his office. As usual, she looked lovely in a long, flowing, black skirt. Her hair was pulled up in a cascade of curls, which sat on top of her head. "Just letting you know I'm leaving for the day."

Terrance broke out in a big smile. Raquel had been quiet pretty much all day. He'd wanted to ask her if everything was all right, but he'd had to rush into a meeting, and after that Savannah had shown up to bring him lunch, which she'd started doing regularly, even though he'd told her not to.

"Hey, before you go, I just wanted to ask how things were going. How are you doing?"

Raquel looked down at the floor, then back up at him. "I'm fine."

Terrance looked at her knowingly. "How long have we been friends?"

Raquel tried to smile. "I don't know about friends, but I've been working for you for three years."

"And you've been my friend for all three of those years, would you say that's correct?"

She nodded.

"And you know I can tell when you're not being straightforward with me. So I'll ask again, and you know it's against God's law to lie in church," he playfully warned.

She chuckled. "Yeah, right. If that were the case, then half the people in this church are in trouble."

He smiled.

"No, I'm okay, really. Just more problems with Dolan, but nothing I can't work through." She tried to shoot him a reassuring look. He definitely wasn't convinced.

"What happened to you leaving?"

"I'm working on it." She looked away. "But honestly, we had a long talk. He's agreed to take anger-management classes and, well, we'll just see . . ."

Terrance couldn't believe she was even contemplating staying with that fool.

"I have to ask this, has he hurt you again?"

She shook her head. "No, it's just that I'm torn. I was very much in love with Dolan. But I just don't know anymore. And even though he's really trying, with each day that passes, I'm wondering more and more what I ever saw in him."

Terrance was silent a few minutes before saying, "Well, you know if you ever need anything, don't hesitate to let me know."

"What about you?" she asked, obviously trying to change the subject. "You and Savannah seem to be spending more time together."

"It's okay. She's not as bad as people think, but I don't know if it's anything serious."

"Umph, you know your aunts try to pump me for information almost daily."

"Why does that not surprise me?" Terrance was grateful that, if nothing else, Raquel was loyal, and he didn't have to worry about her telling any of his business.

"So you think you'll propose to her in time for the Christmas celebration?"

Terrance's eyes grew wide. "Whoa, don't even go there."

Raquel leaned against his doorway. "You know that's what people around here are talking about."

"Well, seeing as how the celebration is only two months away, I doubt very seriously that I'll be giving them what they want."

"They'll have to settle for you just having a girlfriend, huh?" She seemed to be waiting on him to confirm that Savannah was indeed his girlfriend.

Instead, Terrance just laughed and said, "We'll have to see what happens."

chapter 25

Was that really his phone ringing at this ungodly hour? Terrance fumbled for the phone on the nightstand next to his bed. He managed to open his eyes, and all he saw was the red digital alarm clock blaring 3:15 a.m.

"Hello," he mumbled, hoping nobody had died, since those were the only kinds of calls he ever got this time of morning.

"Hello?" he repeated when the caller didn't respond. He heard whimpering.

"Terrance? I mean, Pastor Ellis?"

"Raquel?" he asked, sitting up in his bed.

"Yeah, it's me," she said, sniffing.

"What's wrong?" He felt his heart speed up.

"I'm so sorry to call you this late, but . . ."

"Don't apologize. Tell me what's wrong."

"I . . . I left. I left Dolan."

Terrance was fully awake now. For Raquel to be calling him this time of morning meant something was seriously wrong. "What did he do?"

"He hit me again and I'm not living like that. When I told him that, he . . . he got even more violent, so I left," she softly cried.

"Where are you? Are you in your car?"

"He hid my keys, and the spare. So, I left on foot. I just wanted to get out of there. I've never seen him like that."

"Oh, Raquel, where are you?" Terrance asked, throwing back the covers on his bed. "I'm on my way."

"I'm at the IHOP restaurant near Meyerland." He could feel the relief in her voice. "I just walked to the first open restaurant I could find."

"Well, go inside and wait. I'll be there in fifteen minutes."

"Terrance?"

"Yeah?" He was already slipping into his jogging pants.

"Thank you."

"I told you, anything for a friend. I'm on my way." He hung up the phone, grabbed his keys, and darted out.

Twenty minutes later Terrance was sitting in a booth across from Raquel.

"So, are you sure it's over?" he asked. When he'd shown up, Raquel had hugged him so tightly, it made his heart hurt. Her eyes were red and puffy, her hair was disheveled, and she looked like she'd been to hell and back.

"I'm positive. I've been trying to hang in there, but I just can't do it anymore." She sounded like a wounded animal, and he wanted more than anything to take her in his arms and ease her pain. The way he was feeling actually shocked him. He'd always cared for Raquel, but this felt different. Seeing her so unhappy touched him deeper than he thought it would.

"I hate to have to call you like this, but I tried to call the police on Dolan and he just went ballistic," Raquel said, her voice full of sadness.

"That's insane. What did he expect you to do? Just sit there and let him beat you?" Terrance huffed.

"I know, but Dolan isn't exactly a rational thinker."

Terrance fought back the urge to hunt Dolan down and show him what it felt like to get beat. "Did the cops ever come?"

Raquel fought back tears as she seemed to replay the last few hours in her mind. "He yanked the phone out of the wall before I could even connect the call."

Terrance reached out and covered her hands with his. "Raquel, I'm so sorry. You are a wonderful woman. You don't deserve that."

She dabbed at her eyes. "I know I don't. I just hate that it took me so long to realize that."

He didn't know what to say, so he said, "Remember Second Corinthians, twelve and ten, 'When I am weak, then He is strong.' "

She smiled. "Always the pastor, huh?"

He shrugged and returned her smile. "Can't help it."

They continued talking, and before Terrance knew it, the sun was coming up. "Wow, look at the time. I know you've got to be tired."

She yawned. "Actually, I am worn-out." She reached for her purse. "If you can just drop me off at the nearest hotel, I'll be fine."

"Hotel?" He looked at her like she was crazy. "You are not going to a hotel."

"And where else would I go?"

"You're going to my place until you get back on your feet," he replied, like it was the only viable option.

"Oh, Terrance, I can't do that. I'll figure something out."

"It's already figured out." He stood and extended his hand. "I have a three-bedroom townhome. I'm hardly ever there. I will be highly insulted if you don't let me utilize those paisley sheets Aunt Eva bought for my guest room." He plastered a fake offended look across his face. "And do you know how much a hotel bill will run you?" Terrance added, trying to convince her.

"But what about Savannah?" Raquel finally said.

Honestly, Terrance hadn't even thought about Savannah. She definitely wouldn't like Raquel staying at his place, but it was his place. "You let me worry about Savannah, okay?"

She gently smiled as she stood and took his hand. "Okay."

"Now let's go home." He led her out of the restaurant.

chapter 26

Count to ten. Do not go off. Savannah had to repeat the mantra over and over in her head. She wanted to lose it after hearing Terrance tell her Raquel would be staying with him for a little while.

Technically, she couldn't really say anything because they hadn't formally committed. Shoot, besides the one time they'd made love, they hadn't really done anything but hung out, having a good time. But she hadn't been patient for nothing. She'd been trying to show Terrance she could be his friend as well as his woman. Raquel moving in would definitely throw a monkey wrench in her plan.

"Hello, Savannah, are you still there?" Terrance said into the phone.

Savannah took a deep breath and snapped back to her phone conversation. "Yeah, I'm still here. I just don't understand why she has to stay with you," she whined.

"Well, I've already explained. She's a friend, number one. Number two, she has nowhere else to go."

Think, think, think, Savannah tried to tell herself.

"I understand that this may be difficult for you, but you have to know I'd be this way with anyone in need," Terrance continued.

Yeah, but Raquel ain't just anyone, Savannah wanted to scream. She's the type of woman everyone wanted him with. Savannah finally deduced that she would just have to step up her game. If she went off, it would only turn Terrance off, and since she wasn't officially his girlfriend, she couldn't risk that.

She softened her tone. "I understand that. That's the type of man you are. And that's what I love about you." Terrance was silent, like her profession of love had thrown him off. But she had purposefully said that, throwing it in to solidify her position. "And, no, I don't like the idea of another woman laying up in your house—"

Terrance cut her off. "She'll be in the guest room."

"But," Savannah continued before he could cut her off again, "you are her friend, and if a person can't count on their friends, who can they count on?" Savannah wanted to play the sensitive, understanding role and show him what a good sport she was.

Terrance hesitated again before saying, "Wow, Savannah. You took this a lot better than I thought you would."

"Terrance, I know people have said all these horrible things about me, but I really am a good person," she sweetly replied.

He hesitated. "I know you are, Savannah. That's why I care about you so much."

It was her turn to pause. It wasn't quite what she

wanted to hear; after all, she had just told him she loved him. The night they'd made love, he'd told her he loved her. But it *was* in the heat of the moment when he'd said it. And after she'd asked him three times to tell her he loved her. She'd been hoping he'd repeat it over the last three weeks, but so far, not a word.

"Well, Terrance, you let me know if I can help in any way. If she needs someone to talk to, you know, another female perspective, I'd love to come to talk to her. Lord knows I've had my share of no-good men." Savannah immediately grimaced. Maybe she shouldn't have said that. It would only remind Terrance that she'd been around.

Terrance didn't pay her comment any attention, because he quickly bid her good-bye and made his way downstairs into the living room. Raquel was sitting on the sofa, already engrossed in a movie on the Lifetime Movie Network.

"Oh, no," Terrance said, sitting down in the oversize chair across from her. "Didn't you get the memo? There is a no-Lifetime rule in this house."

"Then I'd better leave right now." She laughed.

He loved her laugh. It was infectious and could brighten up the darkest of rooms. He marveled at how comfortable she looked curled up on the sofa. She looked like she belonged there. Like she was right at home. Terrance shook his head, trying to get rid of the strange feelings that were starting to creep up on him whenever he was around Raquel.

"How long you been up?" he asked.

"A couple of hours." She pulled a burgundy afghan throw up to her chest. "I couldn't really sleep."

The smile left Terrance's face. "Are you sure you're gonna be okay?"

She nodded, then turned to him, her eyes filling with tears again. "It's just sad to see your dreams go up in smoke. But I know God doesn't make mistakes, and He revealed to me that Dolan was not the man for me." She let out a long sigh. "Even still, I hate that I've wasted six years of my life. I mean, I'm not getting any younger you know. And who the heck wants to start over in this dating game?"

"Ain't that the truth." Terrance thought back to his last few disastrous dates. "I think that's why I kinda settled with Savannah. The whole dating thing is not for me."

Raquel looked uneasily at him.

"What?"

She shrugged. "I don't know. Honestly, I really didn't see Savannah as being for you either," Raquel softly replied. "It kind of surprised me that you were with her."

"You and everybody else. But she's a lot better than people give her credit for. In fact, she was even okay with you staying here, offering help if you needed it."

"Did she really?"

Terrance nodded. "That's the sweet side of her that no one ever sees."

"Well, I hope she makes you happy."

They sat in comfortable silence for a few minutes, with Terrance even finding himself drawn into the Lifetime movie.

"You'd better not ever tell anyone that I spent the

morning watching Lifetime," he playfully threatened after the movie went off.

She laughed. "Scout's honor."

They spent the rest of the day just lounging around the house, talking, dozing off and on, and scrounging around for something to eat. It was the first time since Terrance could remember that he just spent a leisurely day doing nothing.

Finally, as the sun began to set, Terrance told her, "I'd better go call Savannah back and then work on my sermon for tomorrow." Savannah had called seven times throughout the day, each time with a different excuse about what she wanted. He eventually told her he'd just call her back when he got a chance.

"How about I whip up some chicken Alfredo while you work?" Raquel suggested. "Provided you have all of the ingredients."

"Well, I know I have chicken and even the pasta, but I don't know about the Alfredo sauce."

"Oh, I make my own Alfredo sauce." She stood, then leaned over and gently kissed him on the head. "Thanks for everything, Terrance. I'll have dinner ready in about an hour."

Terrance smiled up at her. "Hmmm, beautiful, smart, nice, *and* you make Alfredo sauce from scratch? Where have you been all my life?" he said jokingly. But as she playfully waved him off and walked into the kitchen, he felt a small twinge in his heart that had him really wishing that he wasn't joking.

chapter 27

Terrance stared at the light fixture as it hung loosely by its cord from the ceiling.

"Do I need to make a run for it?" Raquel asked as she leaned against the doorframe.

"Look, don't you know that I'm a jack-of-all-trades?" He held up the screwdriver and playfully shook it at her. "I told you I'd get this ceiling fan installed, and doggone it, I'm going to get it installed."

She shrugged. "Sorry, I just thought you meant you'd get it installed today."

"Oh, you got jokes." Terrance cocked his head and studied the many wires hanging out of the ceiling. The guest room where Raquel was staying sat on the west side of the townhome, and the sun made it hot in there, so Terrance had told Raquel he'd install her a ceiling fan.

Raquel laughed as she shook her head. "Terrance, why is it so difficult for you to admit that you don't know what in the world you're doing?"

"Why don't you have any faith in me?" He pulled

on one of the wires. "I told you that all you had to do was—" He jumped back. "Ouch!" he screamed after several sparks shot from the wires. He jerked his hand back and quickly stuck his fingers in his mouth. "Man, that hurt," he mumbled.

"Are you trying to kill yourself?" Raquel sighed as she walked over and extended her hand toward Terrance. "Get down off the ladder. I told you, it's no big deal. I will buy a little portable fan for the room until you can get a professional to come in and install the ceiling fan the right way."

"I told you I could do it," he said as he eased off the ladder.

"Obviously, you can't." She took his hand. "Look, you've burned yourself. Come on, let me find something to put on that."

Raquel led Terrance back to the bathroom. "Where's your first-aid kit?"

Terrance, who had gone back to sucking on his fingers, used his elbow to point toward the sink. Raquel opened the cabinet doors and began sifting through all of the junk under the bathroom sink. She found the first-aid kit, pulled it out, opened it, then removed some burn cream. "Come here," she said.

Terrance knew he was probably acting like a baby right now, but truthfully, it felt wonderful to have someone take care of him. Granted, Raquel always watched out for him and had his back, but this time, things seemed different.

"Let me see your hand." Raquel inspected his hand. Small blisters had begun to form on the tips of three of his fingers. "Dang, you got burned pretty bad."

Terrance watched as she went to work. She eased his hand under the faucet, running some cool water over it. Then she pulled it back, dried it off, and began applying burn cream to his fingers.

"There, is that better?" she asked after she had gently massaged the cream into his fingers.

"Much better." Terrance smiled. Raquel was standing right in front of him. "My faithful assistant. I should've known you'd make things better."

"Yeah, good ol' dependable Raquel. You can always count on her to make things better," she quipped.

Terrance's expression turned serious. "I didn't mean it like that."

She laughed. "I know." Raquel was silent for a minute as she stared at him with an intensity he'd never seen before. "I like making things better for you, Terrance," she said, her voice soft and low.

Terrance felt goose bumps creep up his back. He didn't understand what was going on. Raquel was just a dear friend. That's all. *So, why are you suddenly so nervous around her?* he silently asked himself.

"Thank you," he finally managed to say. The next thing Terrance knew, he had leaned in and gently kissed Raquel on the lips. At first she tensed up, but then, her body began to relax. Her eyes were closed, but Terrance could feel the intensity in her kiss.

After about a minute, Raquel must've caught herself because she pulled back and stared at Terrance.

Terrance didn't know how to read her reaction, so he immediately apologized. "I . . . I'm sorry. I don't know what I was thinking."

Raquel shook her head like she was trying to make

sure she hadn't imagined the whole thing. "Ummmm, I think we both just got carried away for a minute," she said, backing up.

Terrance wanted to kick himself. He didn't know where that had come from. They were friends. Shoot, he was her boss. He couldn't believe that he'd kissed her.

"Yeah, you're right."

He glanced down at his hand. "Thanks for fixing me up. I think I'm going to head to bed now. I'm kind of tired."

"Yeah, me, too." They stood staring at each other awkwardly before Raquel headed toward the door.

"Raquel?"

"Huh?" she replied, turning around.

"Are we okay? I mean, I'm really sorry. I didn't mean to . . . you know . . ."

"We're okay. Don't worry about it. We're both just vulnerable right now. I know you didn't mean anything by it." She tried to smile before making her way out of the bathroom.

Terrance wanted desperately to stop her, to tell her that he did really mean it. But instead, he just let her walk out.

As soon as she was gone, Terrance turned on the faucet in the shower. If ever he needed a cold shower, it was now.

chapter 28

"Okay, I'm straight about to lose my cool," Savannah griped to Tyra as she slammed the phone down. "It's been two freaking weeks and I haven't spent any time with Terrance! If it wasn't for me going to church, I wouldn't see him at all. Oh, but you'd better believe little Miss Purity sees him every day!"

"Dang, girl, calm down," Tyra said, munching on some Pringles.

Savannah paced back and forth across the living room in their apartment. "I can't calm down. I *won't* calm down. I'm sick of playing this understanding-girlfriend role."

Tyra held up a finger. "Ummm, technically, you're not his girlfriend."

Savannah cut her eyes at her friend. "Shut up, Tyra."

Tyra shrugged and went back to her Pringles.

"All I'm saying," Savannah continued as she plopped down on the sofa, "is I'm tired of being this patient, sweet girl. It's one thing to be understanding about that woman staying with him. But it's another when she starts taking time away from me."

Tyra narrowed her eyes in confusion. "You really were never understanding, Savannah. You just knew you didn't have a choice."

"You know, you're really not helping."

"I'm sorry," Tyra said, finally turning serious. "I know you're upset, but what good is that doing you? Shoot, you're losing your edge anyway. If it had been me, I would've been over there two weeks ago. We all woulda been sitting up in his living room like one big happy family."

Savannah threw up her hands in frustration. "So, what am I supposed to do, just show up at his front door?"

Tyra shook her head like she couldn't believe Savannah wasn't getting it. "Yeah. Girl, you're resourceful. You better come up with an excuse and get your tail over there before she plays up that oh-my-man-beat-me-and-I-need-your-big-strong-arms-to-protect-me act." Tyra shot Savannah a no-nonsense look that seemed to say, *What are you waiting for, go.*

"You're right," Savannah finally said as she stood up.

Tyra frowned. "But, I'm gonna need you to go change out of that frumpy-looking outfit and go put on something cute."

Savannah looked down at her oversize sweatshirt and black leggings. "You got a point." She laughed. "Let me go get cute."

"And hurry up," Tyra called after Savannah as she hurried to her bedroom to change.

Thirty minutes later Savannah was knocking on Terrance's door. It was ten o'clock, so she figured he was finished writing his sermon. She had a toothbrush and change of clothes stuffed down in her large Hobo bag. Since it was already so late, she was hoping that she'd be able to spend the night.

Savannah was just about to knock again when the door swung open.

"Savannah?"

Savannah had to catch herself because she knew she had a crazy look on her face. "Raquel. I didn't expect you to answer the door." Raquel looked extremely comfortable with her hair pulled back in a ponytail, in a pair of lounging pants and a T-shirt that read WHAT WOULD JESUS DO?

"Terrance is in his office. I was in the living room watching television and told him I'd get the door," Raquel said, sounding chipper.

Savannah reached up and pushed the door, nearly knocking over Raquel as she made her way in. "How thoughtful of you. I just wanted to stop by and check on Terrance. I know he's been under a lot of pressure lately, and I was worried about him."

"Oh, okay. Well, I'll let him know you're here."

Savannah spun on Raquel. "I can let him know myself." She wasn't trying to be downright rude, but she didn't like how Raquel was making her feel like *she* was the one intruding.

"Have it your way," Raquel said, throwing up her hands, the pleasantness gone from her voice.

Terrance must've heard them talking because he appeared in the living room. "Savannah? I thought I heard your voice. What are you doing here?"

Savannah glared at Raquel, then turned toward Terrance, a smile immediately filling her face. "Hi, sweetie. I just wanted to bring you some of your favorite." She held up the Baskin-Robbins ice cream bag, glad that she'd thought at the last minute to stop. "Rainbow sherbet. I know you've been kind of stressed."

Terrance didn't look the least bit happy to see her. "You should've called."

She bit her lip. "Well, I was just running to the drugstore and thought about you while I was out. I didn't have my cell phone," she said, silently praying that the dang thing didn't start ringing in her purse. "I really didn't think it would be a problem."

Terrance sighed. "I'm sorry. I didn't mean it like that. We were just about to head to bed."

Savannah raised her eyebrows. "We?"

Terrance shook his head. "You know what I meant."

Savannah folded her arms, attitude slowly settling in. "No, enlighten me."

"I meant *we,* as in me in my bed and Raquel in hers. Don't try to make this out to be something it's not."

Savannah glanced over at Raquel, then back at Terrance. "You know, Terrance, I can't really tell what it is. Ever since she weaseled her way in here, you don't seem to have time for me anymore."

Raquel must finally have decided to step in. "Look, Savannah, I hope you don't think I'm here to cause any problems. I was ju—"

Savannah held up her hand, cutting Raquel off. "Look, ain't nobody talking to you. This is between me and my man."

"Savannah, please don't come over here starting any

mess." Terrance sighed. "Raquel's been through enough."

Savannah dramatically rolled her eyes. "Oh, forgive me. *Raquel's* been through a lot. *Raquel* has had a hard time. I'm so glad everybody's so doggone concerned about Raquel."

"You know what? I think you need to leave," Terrance said firmly.

"*I* need to leave? *I* need to leave? I'm your woman. If anybody should be leaving, it needs to be her," Savannah spat.

"Terrance, I'm so sorry. I'll go to a hotel," Raquel interjected. "I never meant to cause you any problems."

"Yeah, why don't you go do that. The Motel 6 right down the road had a vacancy sign."

"Savannah!" Terrance admonished. After all the praises he'd been singing about Savannah, he couldn't believe she was over here acting a ghetto-fabulous fool. "You have no right to come into my home demanding who can and can't stay here! I'm going to ask you again, please leave. We'll discuss this another time."

Savannah caught herself, realizing she was actually about to blow everything she'd worked so hard for. Suddenly, she let out a huge sob. "I'm so sorry, Terrance," she cried as she dropped down on the sofa. "I'm just so stressed. I don't know what to do. I came by hoping to talk to you. I've been going crazy."

Terrance's anger seemed to be evaporating. He'd never seen Savannah cry and definitely didn't like the sight of it. "What's wrong?"

Savannah dabbed at her eyes as she tried to taper her tears, which were flowing hard and heavy now. "I, I just don't know how to say this," she said, finally catching her breath.

"Say what?"

Savannah looked over at Raquel, her eyes filled with tears. "Raquel, I'm sorry for acting so ugly toward you. Can you give us a minute?"

Raquel nodded. She wore a look like she was still unsure whether to believe Savannah, but she walked upstairs.

"Terrance," Savannah began after Raquel had left the room. She paused, like she was trying to gather her thoughts together. "I just really don't know how to say this to you."

"Just say it," Terrance said, worried because he had never seen her like this.

"I'm pregnant."

Terrance had to blink a few times to make sure he'd heard her right. "Pregnant?"

She slowly nodded. "I was on the pill but I hadn't been taking them regularly for the past year because I hadn't been sexually active, and it wasn't really a priority for me. I just never thought . . ." She buried her head in her hands and cried.

"Pregnant?" he repeated. "Oh my God. Are . . . are you sure?"

Savannah nodded again as she looked up at him. "Two home tests and a blood test at the doctor's office sure."

Pregnant? Terrance had to sit down himself. He stared at her in utter disbelief. He was the minister of a growing, thriving church. What would he look like getting a woman pregnant and having a baby out of wedlock?

Savannah must've been reading his mind because she said, "I'm not asking for anything from you. I debated having an abortion, but honestly, I just couldn't bring myself to do that. So, I decided I'm just going to move away and have my baby."

Terrance got up and began pacing the room, trying to compose his thoughts. Abortion definitely wasn't an option. But neither was her moving away and his pretending like he didn't have a kid. He would never subject his child to something like that.

"Terrance, I'm soooo sorry." Savannah's sobs became more intense.

Terrance sat back down next to her, taking her hand. "Sssshhh, don't cry," he said, stroking her hair. "You didn't do this by yourself so you're not going to deal with it by yourself."

She lay on his chest. She seemed comforted by his touch. Terrance, on the other hand, felt like his world was starting to fall apart.

chapter 29

Terrance stood in the doorway watching Savannah drive off. He was grateful for her leaving because after the bombshell she'd just dropped, he needed some time to get his head together.

"Are you okay?"

Terrance turned toward Raquel, who had reappeared in the entrance to the den. "Oh, yeah, I'm fine."

She walked over and stood in front of him. "Terrance, I know you're trying to do the honorable thing by giving me a place to stay, but really, I can go find a hotel, or someplace to go. I don't want to be causing any problems."

"You're not causing any problems." Terrance looked at Raquel. She was visibly concerned that her presence was creating problems. The more he looked at her, the more he knew that he had to let her know what was going on.

"Have a seat, Raquel." Terrance put his hand in the small of her back and led her toward the sofa.

Raquel looked uneasy as she sat down. "What's going on? I mean, you don't have to sugarcoat the fact that you need to put me out. I said I'll leave."

"Nobody is putting you out." Terrance sat down next to her on the sofa. This had to be one of the toughest things he'd ever had to do. "Although you may want to leave on your own after you hear what I have to say."

For a brief moment, he contemplated not saying anything to Raquel about Savannah's pregnancy. But he knew she would be crushed to find out some other way. And a part of him felt like she had a right to know.

"I've really enjoyed having you here these last few weeks," Terrance began.

"I've enjoyed being here. But, Terrance, what are you trying to say?"

Terrance inhaled, gathering up his nerves. "You are welcome to stay as long as you need. But, well, as my very dear friend, there's something I feel like you need to know."

Raquel slowly blinked her eyes several times. "This doesn't sound good. I think I know what it is. You want to make things work with Savannah. I understand and respect that." She sounded like she was trying to convince herself.

"I think I'm slowly beginning to realize that Savannah is not the woman I want to be with," Terrance stoically said.

"What does that mean?"

Terrance shook off the daze he had found himself

drifting off into. "Nothing. I'm just saying, I don't believe in my heart that she's the one."

Raquel kept the skeptical look on her face. "Then what's going on?"

Terrance squeezed her hand, then stood and walked to the other side of the room, his hands stuffed in his pockets. "I really value our friendship."

Raquel stood and followed him across the room. "So do I. However, I feel like there's a *but* coming," she said to his back.

Terrance let out a long sigh. "But . . ."

"Just spit it out, Terrance." Raquel twisted her hands together nervously. "This is killing me. Just say what you have to say."

Terrance turned back to face Raquel, inhaled, then said, "Savannah is pregnant."

Raquel's eyes grew wide and her mouth dropped open.

"I don't know how it happened." Terrance rushed his words out. "I mean, I know, but this is something I never in my wildest dream ever imagined."

Raquel eased back down on the sofa. She shook her head from side to side. "Wow. I don't believe this. Savannah's pregnant."

"It was a mistake," Terrance said desperately. He was surprised that he felt the need to explain, or rather justify himself. Maybe it was the look of pain that shot through her eyes just now. Or maybe it was the unspoken feelings that seemed to be lingering between them.

Tears began to form in Raquel's eyes. "Let me guess. She's pregnant and you have to do what's right?"

"I do. I know people have babies out of wedlock all the time these days. But I can't do that. I have to marry her." He hadn't even discussed marriage with Savannah, but if she was carrying his child, that's the only option he had.

Raquel nodded knowingly. "Of course." She stood. "I wish you and . . ." She paused to compose herself. "I wish you and Savannah the best." She started walking toward the guest bedroom. "Give me a couple of hours and I can have my stuff packed and out of here."

Terrance reached out and grabbed her arm. "Raquel, I told you, you don't have to leave."

Raquel snatched her arm away and flinched. She looked like she was shaking as she fought back tears. "No, I need to leave," she calmly said.

Terrance stepped closer to her. "Please don't leave like this," he whispered.

Raquel glared at him, tears filling her eyes. "What would you suggest I do, Terrance? Do you want me to break out the cigars? Do you want me to plan the baby shower?" She raised her voice. "One minute you're telling me you don't think she's the one. The next, you're talking about marrying her. Am I supposed to be happy about this?"

Terrance was taken aback by her outburst. He looked at her in shock. "I . . . I'm sorry."

She closed her eyes and inhaled. "No, I'm sorry," she said once she opened her eyes back up. "It's just . . . I was hoping . . . I thought . . ." The tears she had been fighting back came pouring out. "I don't know what I thought."

Terrance reached out and took her in his arms. At first, Raquel resisted, but then as the sobs overcame her, she let her body fall limp in his embrace. As he hugged her tightly, Terrance couldn't help but feel like his heart was breaking in a million little pieces, and he began to shed some tears of his own.

chapter 30

Terrance could barely make it through his sermon today, especially with Savannah sitting in the front row, in a short, lavender two-piece suit and matching hat, beaming like she'd been a first lady for all of her life.

He couldn't get Raquel's look of disappointment out of his head. It had haunted him all night. He had convinced her that it was too late to leave last night, so she'd gone to bed, but she was up and gone by the time he'd awakened. He had taken comfort that her stuff was still there. While he was trying to do right by Savannah, he didn't want to just leave Raquel stuck out.

"Hey, baby. What are we eating for dinner today?" Savannah asked after Terrance had said good-bye to the last member. She reached out and straightened his tie. He couldn't help but notice how she said "we," like it was a given that they'd be dining together. His aunts stood off to the side, giving him evil looks, no doubt upset with the way Savannah was fawning all over him. He was in no mood to deal with them today, so as soon as he saw them heading his way, he turned and made a beeline to his office.

Of course, Savannah was right on his heels, chatting away. He had sat down with her this morning before church and told her that he planned to do right by her and their baby. Of course, she'd been ecstatic and her whole mood had been chipper ever since.

A baby? How had he ended up getting Savannah pregnant? He'd tried his best to live the right way, and the one time he'd slipped up, this had been the consequence?

"Babe, why did you run out the sanctuary?" Savannah asked, taking a seat in front of his desk. "I was trying to see where we were going for dinner."

He exhaled loudly. "Look, Savannah. I have a lot to do. I, um, I have to run by Sister Margaret's and check on her husband."

"I'll come with you."

Terrance wanted to scream *No!* but he caught himself and calmly said, "I'm sorry, I just have a lot on my mind and I need to be alone."

Savannah playfully stuck out her bottom lip. "No, T-baby. I'm sorry. I'm being pushy. I know you have a lot to digest, with our baby and all."

Terrance fought down the sick feeling in his stomach. He had been convinced that marrying Savannah was the right thing to do, but now, just the sound of her voice was irritating the heck out of him. He just wanted to get home. "Thank you for being so understanding."

She stood up, reached over, and gently squeezed his hand. "Just call me Miss Understanding."

Terrance was grateful that she didn't fight him and

left quickly. He wasn't too far behind her, because he didn't want to chance running into his aunts.

After a brief run through the drive-through at Burger King, Terrance pulled back up at his house. He just wanted to get inside, gulp down his Whopper, and try to figure out this mess that had become his life.

He'd just walked in the door at home when he bumped into Raquel. His eyes made their way down to the two suitcases in her hands. "Wh . . . What are you doing?"

She lowered her eyes. "Umm, I'm going to stay with my great-aunt."

"The crazy one who lives in an efficiency in the hood? With all of her cats?"

She shot him a forced smile. "Beggars can't be choosy. Besides, it'll only be for a little while. I found an apartment. They'll have it ready for me at the end of the week."

He reached for her suitcases. "Raquel, you don't have to leave."

She pulled both of the suitcases out of his reach. "Yes, I do." She looked him in the eyes. "I've caused enough problems with you and Savannah." She swallowed. "And now, with a baby on the way, well, you don't need any more problems."

Terrance looked down in shame. "About that . . ."

"Hey, you don't owe me any more explanation."

"No, I need you to know that I wasn't lying to you. I really did like Savannah. But I was conflicted in my feelings about her. So, that's why I told you I wasn't sure she was the one."

"You weren't conflicted enough not to sleep with her."

Terrance sighed. "I've only been with Savannah intimately one time."

"That's all it takes."

"I know that. I just . . ." Terrance eased over to the large window in the corner of his living room. He stared outside, thinking. Finally he said, "I don't know how I got myself into this."

"Well, regardless of how you got here, you're here and you have to deal with it." Her voice had lost its accusatory tone. She now sounded genuinely concerned for him.

"You reap what you sow, huh?" Terrance said, turning back to face her.

Raquel set her luggage down. "Yes, but you're a strong man of God and you'll get through this." She walked over to him, then reached out and hugged him. Although her hug was quick and lacked the warmth it normally had, he savored the sweet smell of her perfume.

"You don't have to leave," Terrance whispered. "Honestly, I don't want you to leave."

Raquel pulled away. She seemed to be trying to gather her strength. "No, I really do need to leave." She hesitated like she had something to say, then changed her mind.

"What?" he asked, reading her eyes.

"Terrance, you are a very special man. You helped me get out of a very bad situation, and for that I thank you. But being here . . . with you. It's not good. Especially now."

They stared at each other, not saying a word. They didn't need to. Her eyes told Terrance she felt the same way about him as he did about her. They had both fallen in love.

chapter 31

"If she's pregnant, so am I." Monty stared at Terrance like he couldn't believe Terrance was buying Savannah's claim. He'd stopped by Terrance's place after visiting some woman he was dating in the neighborhood. They were sitting at the kitchen bar where Terrance had just told Monty the news about Savannah's pregnancy. "I know you're all saved and sanctified and stuff. But everybody ain't, especially that trick you're messing with," Monty continued.

"Stop calling her that."

"She's a trick who's tricking you," Monty casually responded. "I mean, come on, man, she couldn't do no better than a fake pregnancy?"

Terrance had never really given much thought to the idea that Savannah could be making this all up. Until Savannah showed him otherwise, he wanted to give her the benefit of the doubt.

"Tell me, were you all in the middle of an argument when she blurted this news out?" Monty asked.

Terrance thought about it. "Not really. Well, she was a little upset about Raquel being at my house."

Monty threw up his hands. "Oh, gimme a break. Dude, I know it's been a while since you been in the game, but come on. That girl has had one thing on her mind since y'all started dating, snagging you. And she's willing to do it by any means necessary. You need to listen to your boy. I know the sneaky ways of women, and Savannah is straight runnin' game."

"Naw, man. I believe her. I mean, I did sleep with her," Terrance replied with a heavy sigh.

"Yeah, you and probably half the other men in this town."

Terrance cut his eyes at Monty.

"Oh, let me guess, you don't want me bad-mouthing your fake baby mama?"

"And what if she's telling the truth?"

Monty looked like he didn't want to even fathom that scenario. "Shoot, on the rare, rare, rare chance that she's telling the truth, there's no law that says you have to be with her just because she's having your kid."

Terrance looked at his friend, wondering how they even stayed friends, their views were so different. "Number one, I'm not going to run from my responsibility."

"Nobody's saying run from the kid, Terrance, man. Just run from Savannah."

Terrance shook his head. "The other thing is, it's bad enough that I had premarital sex after vowing not to, but what kind of example would I be setting as a minister to have a baby out of wedlock?"

"You're human. Just ask God to forgive you and move on," Monty nonchalantly replied.

"God doesn't work like that. Your remorse has to be real. And, well, I'm just not gon' mess up and say, 'Oh, well, God forgives me.' Forgiveness isn't that simple to me."

Monty sighed, seemingly frustrated that he wasn't getting through to his friend. "So does this mean you plan on marrying this chick?"

"It looks like I don't have much of a choice." Terrance got up and walked over to the refrigerator. He grabbed two Cokes. "Want one?" he asked, holding the drinks up to Monty.

"Dog, marrying Savannah is a bad decision," Monty said, taking one of the sodas. "And what about Raquel?"

Just hearing Raquel's name tore at Terrance's heart.

"Last time I talked to you, you were talking about how you were feeling her and everything," Monty continued.

"I was. I am," Terrance replied dejectedly as he sat back down on the barstool and popped the top on his Coke.

Monty leaned over and looked Terrance in the eye just as Terrance was about to take a drink. "Man, is that a look of love? Are you in love?"

Terrance set the can down, leaned back, and rubbed his forehead. "I am in love with Raquel. But it doesn't matter because I have to do right by Savannah."

Monty sat back and opened his drink. "So you give up love because you gotta pay the consequences of one night of lust?" he asked, then took a sip.

Terrance looked away. "Come on, Monty. Savannah isn't that bad." He didn't know whom he was trying to convince, himself or Monty.

"Really she is. And she dang sure ain't no Raquel. She may be finer than Raquel, but that's about it."

"Well, again, it doesn't matter. Savannah is the one pregnant with my child."

Monty shook his head in disbelief. "I can't believe that 'I'm pregnant' trick still works in this day and age. So you're just gon' let Raquel go? Just like that?"

"I don't have a choice."

"Yes, you do. You're just making the wrong one."

Terrance stood and walked over to his bay window. He paused as he gazed outside and took in the beautiful November day. "I don't expect you to understand. No one understands," he finally said. "I grew up without a father. I will not do that to my child."

"Your daddy died before you were even born."

Terrance thought back to the only memory he had of his father—a five-by-seven photo of his father rubbing his mother's pregnant stomach. His father had died in an automobile accident one month before his mother gave birth to him. "I know that," Terrance finally responded. "But I still missed him. I needed him. It's why I was so much trouble growing up. I didn't have any male direction. I won't subject my child to that. I made a promise to God after my grandmother died that I would try to live right. I have some skeletons in my closet as it is. The least I can do is try to honor my word. I . . ." He let his words trail off, not wanting to travel down that painful road again.

"We all got skeletons. And I'm sure your grandmother wouldn't have wanted you to marry a woman you don't love. But you know what?" Monty said, standing and grabbing his keys. "I don't even know why I'm having this conversation with you because homegirl ain't even pregnant."

Terrance was tired of arguing. He'd hoped to find some solace by talking to Monty, but now he felt worse than he did before his friend even arrived.

"I know you're not trying to hear me," Monty said as he headed to the door. "Just whatever you do, don't marry the girl until the baby pops out. And even then, wait for a DNA test!" Monty called out, then the door slammed closed.

chapter 32

Eva couldn't get Thanksgiving dinner out of her mind. She'd been thrilled when Terrance showed up at her door yesterday. That was until she saw Savannah by his side.

"I hope I'm making this very clear," Terrance had said after Eva had tried to talk to him in the kitchen shortly after his arrival. "If you want to be a part of my life, you will have to learn to accept Savannah."

Eva had warned her sisters to be on their best behavior, but as she had stood in the doorway and watched Savannah poised next to Terrance like she was already the first lady, Eva knew she'd be hard-pressed to follow her own advice.

They'd eaten dinner in virtual silence, with Terrance and Savannah both trying to make small talk. Eventually, the two of them left, and Eva and her sisters had been in a funk ever since.

"He is a grown man," Eva had finally conceded to her sisters. They'd been rehashing the dinner as they wrapped up a Christmas committee meeting at the church. Eva and Mamie were still in the conference room, lamenting the situation with their nephew. Dorothy Mae had gone down the hall to the restroom. "We just have to let him make his own mistakes," Eva added.

Mamie stared at her eldest sister like she couldn't believe Eva was throwing in the towel.

"You're kidding, right?" Mamie asked, astonished.

Eva sighed in frustration. "What do you suggest, Mamie? We've dang near run the boy off already. Maybe we just need to let him see what kind of woman Savannah is on his own. I mean, even if she tries to put on an act, eventually her true colors will show. Sooner or later she'll have to scratch her fleas."

Mamie shook her head like she didn't want to accept that. "You can buy it all you want, but not me. I'm going down to his office and let him know what I really think." She pushed back from her seat and bounced down the hallway.

"Mamie, wait," Eva called out, following her. "Don't go busting up in the boy's office." Eva finally noticed Dorothy Mae with her ear against Terrance's door. "Dorothy Mae, are you eavesdropping on that boy?"

"Sssshhhh." Dorothy Mae waved, her eyes wide.

Both Mamie and Eva looked curiously at their sister. She had a frantic look across her face. They watched her for a few minutes until she finally motioned for them to walk back out in the hallway.

"Who's in there?" Eva asked as soon as they stepped in the hallway. "And why were you all up in their conversation?"

"It was Terrance and Raquel," Dorothy Mae whispered.

"His secretary? What were they talking about that has you all in a tizzy?" Eva asked.

Dorothy Mae shook her head, like she didn't know how to break the news.

"Hel-lo," Mamie snapped when Dorothy Mae didn't respond. "You wanna tell us what's going on?"

Dorothy Mae blew out a deep breath. "They were talking about Savannah."

Mamie rolled her eyes.

"Apparently, she's pregnant. And apparently it's Terrance's baby."

Mamie gasped. Eva clutched her heart and let out a deep moan she steadied herself on the water fountain. "Tell me you're lying," Eva finally whispered.

"I wish I were," Dorothy Mae replied.

"He's sleeping with her?" Eva asked in disbelief.

"I keep trying to tell y'all that boy still got needs," Mamie said, shaking her head. "Lord knows, I just wish he coulda fulfilled them with somebody else."

Eva finally seemed to shake off her shock. "I don't believe it."

Both Mamie and Dorothy Mae stared at Eva.

"I mean, we know she'll stoop to any level to get Terrance. This, this oldest trick in the book, is just that—a trick. She knows if she convinces Terrance she's pregnant, he'll do right by her and marry her. I'd be willing to bet she'd then miraculously lose the baby." Eva's voice had finality about it, like she'd completely figured out Savannah's game.

"So what are we supposed to do, wait until he marries her and see?" Dorothy Mae asked.

"No, I have the perfect plan," Eva announced, her mind racing. "I told y'all, Little Miss Thang just doesn't know who she's messing with."

"I thought you were throwing in the towel," Mamie declared. "Didn't you just tell me to let him find out she wasn't the one for him on his own?"

"No, this little scam of hers changes everything," Eva replied.

"So what are we going to do?" Dorothy Mae asked.

Eva got a sly look. "Oh, believe me, I have it all figured out. It's as simple as a visit. So let's go."

Eva started marching down the hall.

"Where are we going?" Mamie asked, trying to match her sister's stride.

"To pay Miss Thang a visit." Eva was furious. "Savannah is out of her mind if she thinks she's going to trick my nephew. I'm about to show her that when you play with fire, you're bound to get burned."

chapter 33

"I still can't believe we're just going to show up at her doorstep and demand that she take a pregnancy test," Dorothy Mae said as they pulled up in front of Savannah's North Side apartment. They had stopped in the church office, pulled up Savannah's address in the database, and hightailed it over to her place.

"Believe it," Eva said, throwing the car into park.

"So is Terrance really on his way?" Dorothy Mae asked.

"He should be here any minute now," Eva said, glancing at her watch as she got out of the car. "I called him from the drugstore and told him it was imperative that he get over here right away."

"How do you know she's even home?" Mamie said.

Eva rolled her eyes. "She doesn't work, trifling behind. Where else is she gonna be?"

Eva led the way as they made their way up to Savannah's apartment. She vigorously knocked on the door.

After about five minutes, a groggy Savannah opened the door. "Who is knocking on my door like they don . . ." Her voice trailed off and she quickly became alert. "Ms. Eva? What are you all doing here?" She looked back and forth between each woman.

"May we come in?" Eva coldly asked.

Savannah had a horrible migraine and was not in the mood to deal with any of their mess, but she sighed and stepped aside.

"Look," Eva began after they were all inside Savannah's living room. "We understand that you are claiming, excuse me, that you are possibly pregnant with our nephew's child."

Savannah silently cursed herself for even opening the door. She could already tell this conversation was not about to be pretty. She was two seconds past tired of them and ready to give them a piece of her mind.

Instead, she folded her arms and firmly said, "I am pregnant with Terrance's child."

Eva grimaced. Both Mamie and Dorothy Mae groaned in disgust. "If that's the case, that means you will be a part of our family—whether we like it or not."

Savannah softened her defensive stance. "I guess it does mean that."

"And in the interest of the child, we all should find a way to get along," Eva continued.

Savannah dropped her arms. She seemed relieved. "I couldn't agree more."

Eva slowly reached in her purse and pulled out a small, white plastic CVS pharmacy bag. "And therefore, I'm hoping you'll understand when we ask you to take this." She thrust the bag toward Savannah.

Savannah looked down at the bag, then back up at Eva. "What is that?"

"A pregnancy test," Dorothy Mae replied. "Just so that we're all sure you're really with child."

Savannah looked at them like they were crazy. She'd totally had enough. "You know what? I don't need y'all old behinds to be sure about nothing. This is between me and my baby's daddy."

Eva nearly had a heart attack at the mention of Terrance as a "baby daddy."

"So you can take your stupid test and your meddling behinds out of my house," Savannah continued.

They were interrupted by the sound of knocking on the front door. Savannah turned to the door, irritated that someone else had come to disturb her quiet afternoon.

"That would be Terrance," Eva said, when Savannah didn't move. "I asked him to come here."

Savannah cut her eyes at Eva. "I don't believe you all," she mumbled as she stomped over to the door.

"Savannah," Terrance said, rushing in the apartment. "What's going on? My aunt Eva said I needed to get over here immediately." He stopped when he noticed all three of his aunts in the living room.

"What's going on here?" he asked again, this time looking at each woman.

Savannah slammed her door. "Your aunts are here once again, messing with me."

He stared at the three women. "For the last time, does somebody want to tell me what's going on?"

Eva stepped forward. "All we've done is asked Savannah to take a pregnancy test to prove she's really pregnant. That way, we can welcome her into the family."

"Or show her for the lying, no-good floozy she is," Mamie mumbled.

"Aunt Mamie!" Terrance admonished before turning back to Eva. "This is insane. First of all, how did you find out about the pregnancy? And secondly, what gives you the right to come over here trying to confirm it?"

"It doesn't matter how we found out," Eva replied. "And we want to confirm it because we love you and we want to make sure she is on the up-and-up."

"It's not your place to determine who is on the up-and-up for me!" Terrance shouted, anger registering all across his face.

Savannah smirked and Eva wished she could slap her right then. Instead she took a step toward Terrance and calmly said, "I'm sorry you don't agree with us, baby, but if she really is pregnant, what is the harm in taking the test and proving it to everyone? That way, we can eliminate that doubt—and if you really think about it, you have to have some doubt, too—and we can move forward with welcoming that sweet baby into the world."

Savannah wanted to throw up at the way Eva was trying to pour it on.

Terrance pushed Eva's hands away. "It's not your place to do this!" he yelled. "It's not your business at all."

Savannah finally sighed, walked over, and snatched the test out of Eva's hand. "Forget it, Terrance. It's not even worth all this. I'll take the stupid test and once again prove them wrong," she snapped. "Maybe then, they'll leave me the hell alone."

Terrance reached out and grabbed her arm. "Savannah, you don't have to do this."

Savannah calmed herself down and forced a smile. "I want to, Terrance. I'm tired of this and I just want them once and for all to let this vendetta against me go."

She gently removed his hand from her arm. "Just give me a minute." She glared at Eva, Mamie, and Dorothy Mae one last time before heading to the bathroom.

Terrance sighed as he began pacing back and forth across the room. "I just don't believe this. I really don't."

"I don't believe you were sleeping with her. And without protection?" Eva snarled.

"It's none of your business who I'm sleeping with," Terrance snapped.

"Terrance," Dorothy Mae said, stepping toward him, her voice calm. "We love you to death. It will always be our business."

He let out a groan as he buried his face in his hands. He didn't know what to do about them, but this was the last straw. Silence blanketed the room for the next few minutes until Savannah returned with the pregnancy test and a smirk across her face. "You wanted proof, there's your proof." She flung the test at Eva. It hit Eva in the chest and fell to the floor.

Eva slowly reached down and used the tips of her finger to pick up the test. She almost passed out when she saw the two red lines.

Mamie and Dorothy Mae, who were looking over Eva's shoulder, looked dumbfounded as well.

"Well, what does it say?" Terrance challenged.

None of the women replied.

"It says exactly what I told you it would say," Savannah replied triumphantly. "I'm pregnant. Now, I know the next issue will be if Terrance is really the father. And

I gladly welcome a DNA test." Words couldn't describe the way Savannah felt as she took in the astonished looks on their faces.

Mamie snatched the test out of Eva's hands. "Let me see that." She stared closer at the little stick. "I think I'm going to be sick. Where's your restroom?"

Savannah, still wearing her triumphant smile, pointed toward her bedroom.

As Mamie rushed to the restroom, Terrance faced Eva and Dorothy Mae. His voice was remarkably calm. "This was your last time. Your last time harassing my girlfriend." Eva grimaced at the sound of that. Dorothy Mae rolled her eyes, and Savannah grinned widely. She loved having him refer to her as his girlfriend.

Terrance continued, "As God is my witness, if you don't stay out of my business, I will have no choice but to put you out of my life." Anger filled his face.

Eva looked at him in disbelief. "Terrance, you would turn your back on your own family?"

Terrance held his ground. "If family can't respect my wishes, then yes." He took Savannah's hand. "How Savannah and I handle this situation is our business and our business only. Do you understand?"

Eva, whose eyes seemed to be filling with tears, slowly nodded.

"I am so disgusted and disappointed in your behavior, I don't know what to do," Terrance added. "I think you owe Savannah an apology."

Eva had just opened her mouth when Mamie came bursting out of the bedroom. "Don't apologize! She's a liar. I knew it, I knew it. She's a stone-cold liar. Just like we thought!"

Everyone turned toward Mamie, including Savannah, who no longer wore the smirk across her face.

Mamie held up the pregnancy test in one hand and a red pen in the other. "She drew the line!"

"What?" Eva said, stepping forward.

"That's right," Mamie excitedly replied. "On pregnancy tests the second line is always lighter than or the same color as the test line. I thought something was fishy because the second line was so dang dark. I went in her bathroom, and lo and behold, this was laying on her bathroom counter." She shook the red pen.

"You're insane," Savannah muttered.

"That's ridiculous," Terrance replied. "Haven't you all caused enough trouble? A pen doesn't mean she doctored a pregnancy test."

"Maybe not, but a real positive result wouldn't smear when you run water over it!" Mamie held the test up to Terrance's face.

The second window no longer had two lines, but instead one solid test line and blurred red ink in the place of the second line.

"Oh my God." Dorothy Mae laughed.

"You forget, I used to be a nurse," Mamie triumphantly said. "I know a fake test when I see one."

"Gimme that," Savannah said, snatching the test. "Get out of my house. I've had enough."

Terrance suddenly looked like he didn't know what to believe. He stared at the test, which was tightly clutched in Savannah's hand.

"Terrance, I know you're not going to believe this nonsense," Savannah pleaded. "They're trying everything under the sun to get you to leave me."

Terrance looked down into her hand. "Let me see that."

Savannah moved the test behind her back. "Terrance, don't do this. Your aunt altered the test."

"We do have another one if you'd like her to take it again," Eva said. This time, she was the one smirking. "And one of us could stand watch to make sure she doesn't doctor the test this time."

Savannah could no longer hold it in. She spun on Eva. "Would you shut up? I've never done anything to any of you. Why are you harassing me? I wish all of you would just leave me alone!"

Eva got in her face. "It's such a shame that you have to stoop so low to try and snag a man."

"Maybe I wouldn't have to stoop to anything if you'd keep your nose out of our business and let Terrance be with who he wants to be."

Mamie stepped up to Savannah as well. "So you are saying you did stoop to trying to trick him into thinking you were pregnant."

Savannah looked flustered. "That's not what I'm saying. I was trying to say . . ." She stopped and shook her head. "Get out! Get out now!"

Terrance ignored his aunts and stared at Savannah. "Savannah," he said, his voice firm. "Tell me the truth. Are you or are you not pregnant?"

"Terrance, can we have this conversation after they leave?" Savannah now had tears in her eyes. Everything she'd worked so hard for was crumbling right before her.

"Are you or aren't you?" Terrance bellowed, catching everyone off guard because it was a tone they seldom heard.

Savannah lost it and burst into tears. "I'm sorry. I . . . I thought I was . . . And when I found out I wasn't, you were talking about plans for our future and I . . . I couldn't bring myself to tell you the truth."

She wanted to kick herself. Why did she let her guard down? Why didn't she keep her lie going? "Please understand," she sniffed as she stepped toward him.

Terrance stepped back so she wouldn't touch him. "You lied? You tricked me?"

He backed up toward the door. Eva eased toward him. "Come on, baby. Better you found out now than later," she soothingly said. Terrance snatched away from her as well.

"Leave me alone," he said with a force that frightened her. "All of you, leave me alone." He looked around the room at all four women. "All of you disgust me."

Terrance turned and swung the door open, ignoring the calls of each woman as they begged him to come back.

chapter 34

"It's killing me to not talk to Terrance," Mamie said, her voice laced with sadness. She, Eva, and Dorothy Mae were at Denny's having their regular Wednesday-morning coffee.

"Yeah, it's been almost a week. How long do you think he's going to stay mad at us?" Dorothy Mae said as she added two teaspoons of sugar to her coffee.

Eva shrugged. "I have no idea. Every time I've tried to call or go by his office, he won't even talk to me. Raquel said to just give him some time. That's the only good thing in all of this. Him and Raquel seem to be growing closer."

"You think something's going on?" Mamie asked.

"Well, I heard through the grapevine that they've been spending a whole lot of time together. And truth be told, I think they make the perfect couple. But I wouldn't know if something is really going on. She's very protective of him and I can't get anything out of her, and I dang sure can't get any information about their relationship." Eva sipped her coffee. "Ladies, I think we might have really gone too far this time. I've never seen Terrance like this."

"Well, we'll just have to pray he comes around," Mamie said.

"We're still his family, so he will eventually come around. Besides, we have another issue to worry about," Dorothy Mae added.

"What?" Mamie asked.

"We're just a few weeks away from the Christmas celebration, and I overheard that same old tired argument from the deacons," Dorothy Mae said.

"You sure do a lot of overhearing," Eva snapped.

"Well, it seems to be the only way to find out anything these days," Dorothy Mae retorted.

"Well, what were they talking about?" Mamie asked.

"The usual. Getting rid of Terrance."

"This is just crazy. Terrance is good for this church and they want to get rid of him because he's single," Eva groaned.

"You know most of them are just old school. They think if you're thirty and single, something's wrong. Dang down-low brothers got everybody paranoid," Mamie said.

"So what are we gonna do?" Dorothy Mae asked, looking at Eva.

"Why do you all always think I have all the answers?"

"Because you usually do," Mamie replied.

"Well, I don't this time. I don't know that I can stop them from getting rid of Terrance. Just like I couldn't stop him from being with Savannah." Eva sighed dejectedly.

"Oh, but you did stop him from being with Savannah," Dorothy Mae said. "He may be mad at us now, but eventually, he'll thank us for showing Savannah's true colors."

"I hope you're right, little sister," Eva remarked. "Lord knows, I hope you're right."

Savannah took a deep breath. She was standing outside Terrance's office. She felt like a stalker. She'd sat outside, parked across the street, until she saw that his car was the only one left in the church parking lot.

Terrance wouldn't take her calls since the disaster at her house last week. He wouldn't even give her a chance to explain her side of the story.

Savannah was just about to knock on his office door when she heard voices. *Who else is in there?* she grumbled to herself. Somebody was always in his face. That's why they couldn't ever work on their relationship because they were always surrounded by people.

Savannah paused and looked through the cracked door. She didn't see anyone but Terrance. He was facing the door, on his knees in the middle of the room. His Bible was clutched in his hands and his eyes were closed. He was deep in prayer.

Savannah stepped back. She felt guilty spying on him as he was praying. But something about the intense look across his face drew her back to the door. She strained to hear. Maybe he was asking God for guidance on what to do about her. *Please, God, guide him back to me,* Savannah silently mumbled.

". . . and, Father, I know I come to you almost daily

with this, but I need you to deliver me from my guilt," Terrance prayed.

Deliver him from his guilt. Okay, now he definitely had her interest piqued. She leaned in some more and listened to the rest of his prayer, hoping that no one walked by and caught her eavesdropping.

As Savannah listened, she had to grab on to the doorknob and steady herself. She couldn't believe what she was hearing. Terrance? Carrying something like that? Never in a million years would she have thought he was capable of something like that.

She heard him wrapping up his prayer and she quickly walked away from the door. Now she was torn. Should she go in and let him know what she'd heard or wait a few minutes and act like she'd just arrived.

"No, I need to process all of this," she muttered to herself. "I might be able to use this bombshell to my advantage."

Savannah quickly tiptoed back out the door, her mind racing. She couldn't believe what she'd just overheard. Maybe this was God's way of answering her prayers. She nodded, convinced that it was. And for the first time since Terrance walked out of her life, Savannah felt like they might actually have a chance of working everything out.

chapter 35

Savannah brushed down the waist of her chocolate brown wrap dress, then adjusted the opening so that it would show just enough cleavage to let Terrance know what he was missing, but not enough to be trashy.

She'd stored that little bombshell she overheard two days ago in the "last resort" file and was trying everything to win him back fair and square. He hadn't spoken to her since the whole pregnancy fiasco, other than to reiterate that they were finished.

This was her last attempt to be reasonable with him. He was probably going to be upset with her stopping by his place on a Saturday evening, but this was the only time she knew she could catch him at home. He always dedicated the hours between five and seven to prepare for his Sunday sermon. She'd waited around closer to seven, just to give him time to wrap up. Now that it was just a few minutes before the hour, she was on his doorstep, saying a silent prayer that everything would work out.

Savannah reached up and rang the doorbell. She

waited with anticipation as she heard him fumbling toward the door.

The look across his face when he opened the door was exactly what she was hoping he wouldn't have.

"Savannah, what are you doing here?"

She tried her best to smile. "Hoping you'd found forgiveness in your heart. You know, the forgiveness you preach that we should have for one another."

"I forgive you," he said stoically. "I just don't think it's going to work between us."

"Terrance, you have to understand," she said, beginning the speech she'd rehearsed a thousand times. "I was desperate for you to give me a fair chance, and I knew with all the negativity you were surrounded with, that just wouldn't happen."

He leaned against the doorframe and crossed his arms over his chest. "So you just decided to lie?"

She lowered her eyes but didn't respond.

"Look, Savannah," Terrance huffed in frustration. "What's done is done. There is no need to rehash all of this."

She looked him directly in the eyes. "Can I please come in and talk for a moment?"

"I don't think that's a good idea."

"Please. If you ever had any feelings for me, please. Just give me ten minutes, then I'll leave you alone."

Terrance sighed, then stepped aside and let her in.

Savannah turned to face him as soon as he closed the door. "Tell me you didn't feel anything for me. You might not have truly been in love with me, but you were on your way. I know it. I felt it."

He ran his hands over his head. "Truthfully, I did

have feelings for you. Or I thought I did." Terrance blew an exasperated breath. "Come in the living room and sit down. We do need to talk."

Savannah felt a flutter in her heart. The anger seemed to have disappeared from his body. "Terrance, I can't begin to tell—"

"No," he said, cutting her off. "Let me talk." He sat down next to her and took her hand. "Savannah, you are a very sweet woman. Yes, there were some things that as a minister made me very uneasy, but you know I really did like you. I can even say I felt myself falling in love with you."

"Then what's the problem?" Savannah softly said. "If you want me to change some of my ways, I promise I can work on them."

"No, it's not that." He looked like he was choosing his words carefully. "There is some man out there that will take you just as you are. A man who you don't have to change for."

"But I want you," she said, rubbing his face. She couldn't believe how desperate she was sounding. But she was desperate.

Terrance gently removed her hands. "Savannah, I'm so sorry I ever led you on. But, the more I think about it, it just wouldn't work."

"Why, because of those people at church? I can win them over. Just give me a chance."

Terrance got up and began pacing across the room. "It's not just that." He inhaled. "I've thought long and hard about this. Finding out you lied about the pregnancy is not the real reason it won't work between us.

We don't have a future because, well, it's just that . . . my heart lies with someone else." He looked at Savannah, and it took everything in her power for her not to cry.

"Raquel?"

"Yes." Terrance looked relieved to get that off his chest. "I have always had a special relationship with Raquel, but I think I just tried to deny how I really felt about her. Besides, she was engaged and, well, the timing just wasn't right."

"So, it's right now?" Savannah's voice was a mixture of pain and anger.

"Please understand, this is not something I planned. It just happened. The heart wants what it wants."

Savannah stood and angrily tossed her purse on the table. "Save that Hallmark bull for somebody else. You've wanted that little tramp all along, but she probably wouldn't give you the time of day. Now that she will, you wanna just kick me to the curb," Savanna hissed.

Terrance could tell from the look on Savannah's face that his news wasn't going over too well.

"Savannah, it's not like that. I contemplated whether I should tell you, but I figured I needed to be honest with you—even though you weren't honest with me," he threw in.

"So just like that, we're done?" Savannah asked, ignoring his dig at her.

"It's not just like that," Terrance protested.

"So, Reverend"—Savannah put her hands on her hips—"have you slept with Miss Raquel, too? Or, wait, let me guess. You want to keep her pure and use me to get your rocks off."

"Savannah, you know better than that."

"Do I?" So much for trying to take the sweet approach. "You probably never intended on having a relationship with me in the first place. I was just something to do until Raquel decided she wanted you in her life. I was just a way to get your manly needs fulfilled, is that it? Did the fact that I gave my body to you mean anything?"

Terrance gave her a look to see if she was serious, considering all the men she was rumored to have slept with. He quickly caught himself. None of those rumors had ever been confirmed. And if he didn't believe them before, he knew he shouldn't give them credence now.

"Savannah, I just got caught up in the lust of the flesh. I should have never let that happen."

"But it did happen. And you said you loved me when we made love."

Terrance racked his brain. He couldn't for the life of him remember saying that. But she had been so good in bed, and it had been so long for him, that he was liable to have said anything in the heat of the moment.

"I don't recall saying that, and if I did, I'm sorry. But I care about you, I do."

She blew a disgusted breath. "Whatever. You try to act all holy and stuff, you're nothing but a lying, low-down snake like the rest of the men out there."

Terrance closed his eyes and shook his head.

"Let me explain something to you, Reverend," Savannah began, her voice laced with attitude. "You don't play with a woman's emotions and think it's over just because you say it's over."

"Savannah, please don't make this ugly."

She let out a maniacal laugh. "You've got to be kidding me. Sweetie, trust me when I say things aren't going to get ugly. In fact, they'll be quite beautiful."

Terrance shot her a perplexed look. "What does that mean?"

Savannah flashed him a smile as she headed to the door. "It means, darling, that this"—she pointed between the two of them—"isn't over. In fact, we haven't even begun. I'll be in touch."

Savannah left Terrance looking more confused than ever as she headed back to her car. She hadn't wanted to go this route, but Terrance had left her no choice. It was time for the trump card, the one that would ensure she'd get exactly what she wanted.

chapter 36

"Okay, I'm not understanding this," Tyra said after the waiter had taken their drink orders and left them alone at the small corner table.

"What's there not to understand?" Savannah asked, kicking back in her chair and motioning around the room. They were at the Red Cat, a jazz restaurant in downtown Houston. The place was packed, as usual. "We've got great music, drinks are on the way. We're about to celebrate."

"That's just it. What are we celebrating for? You said Terrance didn't take you back."

"He didn't." Savannah smiled brightly.

"Then why are you grinning like you hit the Lotto or something?"

"I did."

Tyra leaned in and sniffed. "You sure you haven't already been drinking?"

Savannah had been in an unusually happy mood

since she'd called an hour ago and told Tyra to meet her at the Red Cat. Tyra had asked her what had happened at Terrance's, but all Savannah would say was that he reiterated that it was over and that he was pursuing a relationship with his secretary.

Savannah laughed. "Girl, I have not been drinking. Yet. This is a celebration of my soon-to-be life as Mrs. Terrance Ellis and the first lady of Lily Grove Missionary Baptist Church."

Tyra shook her head. "Didn't you say that not only did he refuse to give you another shot, but that he was involved with someone else?"

"Oh, she's nobody." Savannah waved off.

"Savannah McKinney, would you please stop beating around the bush and tell me what's going on," Tyra demanded.

The waiter returned and placed Savannah's apple martini in front of her and Tyra's rum and Coke in front of her. "Will there be anything else?" he asked.

"Not yet," Savannah said. "But please keep our tab open as we'll want to keep the drinks coming."

The waiter nodded and took off. He had just stepped away when a tall, handsome Morris Chestnut–looking man made his way over to their table.

"Excuse me," he said, never taking his eyes off Savannah. "My name is Lance and I was just wondering if I could buy you two ladies a drink."

Tyra displayed a big, cheesy grin. Savannah turned up her nose as she looked him up and down.

"Lance, we can buy our own drinks," Savannah snidely responded. Tyra shot her a confused look.

Lance chuckled. "I'm sure you can. But I was just hoping to, you know, take a moment of your time to get to know you better."

"Well, thanks, but no thanks. We're kinda having a private conversation here," Savannah rudely replied.

Lance nodded, trying not to let his dejection show. "All right. Didn't mean to be a bother. You ladies have a nice evening."

"Have you lost your mind?" Tyra whispered as soon as he walked off. "Did you see how fine he was?"

Savannah dismissed him with a wave of the hand. "Girl, please. I'm not trying to hook up with some dude in the club. I have me a real man." She took a sip of her drink and leaned back.

"Okay, this whole new level of confidence is creepy. The old Savannah would have jumped at the chance to talk to a man as fine as that dude. You need to tell me what is going on."

Savannah looked like she could no longer contain her excitement. "Okay, I guess I won't keep you hanging anymore." She beamed.

"Thank you," Tyra huffed. "Now tell me, why are you so sure that you and Terrance are going to be together? Especially after he told you a hundred times that it's over."

"Because I have an ace in the hole."

"An ace in the hole?"

"That's what I said."

"Well, what is it?"

"Now that, I'm not going to be able to tell you."

Tyra rolled her eyes. "You and all this double-oh-seven spy mess 'bout to drive me crazy."

Savannah laughed. "Seriously, just trust me on this. I have a little secret about the good reverend that will ensure that he will see things my way."

"Ooooh," Tyra said, intrigued. "You playing dirty for real. That's the Savannah I know and love."

"I didn't want to, but he's left me no choice."

"Are you setting him up or something?"

"No, I didn't even have to do anything like that. Let's just say God sent me a little nugget to make all my dreams come true."

Tyra looked like she was deep in thought for a minute. "Savannah, you know you're my girl and I love you, right?"

Savannah nodded. "I know. I love you, too. But why are you saying that?"

"Are you sure that you want to get Terrance this way? I mean, do you really want to blackmail him into being with you?"

Savannah lost her smile. "Really, I don't, Tyra. But I love this man. He's everything I want and need in my life. And I know that he can love me, too. I can be a good wife, if he would just give me the chance. So, no, this isn't the way I wanted to get him to be with me, but I gotta do what I gotta do."

Tyra seemed satisfied with Savannah's answer because she smiled. "I feel you. You do you." She raised her glass in a toast. "To a wonderful future with the man you love."

Savannah clinked her glass with Tyra's.

"And you're not going to tell me this secret for real?" Tyra asked after they both took sips of their drinks.

"Eventually I will. I just can't right now, okay?"

"Cool." Tyra set her drink down. "I say, whatever your plan is, more power to you."

Savannah smiled at her friend. "Thank you, girl. That's why I'm going to let you be in my wedding," Savannah joked.

"Baby, from all the drama you guys have so far, you'd better believe I wouldn't miss the wedding for the world."

They both laughed as thoughts of a life with Terrance filled Savannah's head.

chapter 37

Terrance silently exhaled as he looked up and saw Savannah standing in the doorway of his office. Would she ever give up? He'd tried to end things amicably, but she just didn't seem to want to take no for an answer. He and Raquel had grown even closer over the last two weeks, and he didn't need any unnecessary drama. Dolan was causing enough of that. He'd been stalking Raquel and threatening to make her pay for leaving him. They'd even gone yesterday and gotten an order of protection against him, like that really mattered though because Dolan definitely wasn't the type who cared about a piece of paper. He had Raquel so spooked that she'd taken to sleeping with a knife under her pillow. Terrance had tried to convince her to come stay with him awhile, but she'd settled into her apartment and didn't want to put him out.

"Hello, Savannah," Terrance said, trying to be cordial, but making sure she knew he wasn't exactly greeting her with open arms. For once he found himself wishing

Raquel was at her desk so she could screen his visitors, but she was at a doctor's appointment. Raquel wouldn't have been able to stop Savannah anyway.

"Hello to you," Savannah said, sashaying in. She wore a hot-pink, tight dress that clung to her body and reminded Terrance why she would've never made a proper first lady.

"What can I help you with?" he asked, hoping whatever it was, she'd make it quick. He didn't mean to be so harsh, but he'd tried to take the diplomatic route with her and it just wasn't working.

"How have you been?" she asked, taking a seat in front of his desk.

Terrance set down his pen and looked her directly in the eyes. "Fine. And again, what can I help you with?"

Savannah did a sexy shudder. "Oooooh, so formal." She leaned forward. "There's no need to be so formal, Terrance, especially for someone who's known such intimate parts of me."

Terrance sighed. "Savannah, let's not do this."

"Do what, Pastor?" She batted her eyelashes as she leaned back and crossed her legs. "Oh, let me guess, you're worried that your little girlfriend will come in here and see us," Savannah said when she noticed him looking toward his door, which she had closed when she walked in.

"Savannah, is there a reason you stopped by?" Terrance huffed.

She brushed her dress down as she sat up straight. "Actually, there is." She flashed a devilish smile. "I had hoped you'd fall in love with me willingly."

"Savannah—"

She held up her hand. "Let me finish. Honestly, I think you were on your way, but because of reasons beyond my control, that just didn't happen. So now, I have to take matters into my own hands. I have to take what I can get."

He eyed her suspiciously.

She chuckled. "Let me rephrase that. I guess I will take you however I can."

Now he knew she was crazy. "What is that supposed to mean?"

Her expression turned serious as she lowered her voice and fingered her hair. "It means, when your little secretary bimbo comes back in here, you will inform her that you have decided to give our relationship another chance. And you will give us another chance. You will let everyone at the church know that God has directed you to follow your heart, and your heart lies with me. We will be together, and in time for the Christmas celebration, so you don't have to worry about losing your job," she said matter-of-factly.

Terrance looked at her like she'd lost her mind. She had to have lost her mind. "Excuse me?" he finally muttered.

She leaned back and crossed her legs, making sure her thigh was peeking out of the slit in the dress.

"Are you crazy?" he asked.

"On the contrary. I'm quite sane. I really and truly hate that it had to come to this, but a girl's gotta do what a girl's gotta do."

Terrance had to chuckle himself. "Savannah, you really have lost it. What part of 'It's over between us' don't you get?"

"No part." She shrugged nonchalantly. "Because we're not over." She stood. "I can't wait to see the looks on everyone's faces when they see us together."

"Savannah!" Terrance yelled, hoping to snap her back to her senses. "Are you on some kind of drug? There is no us! There will never be an us."

She smiled again. "Ahhh, but that's where you're wrong, boo. You wanna know why you're wrong?" She was toying with him now and enjoying every minute of it. She had to show him that she wasn't one to be played with.

Terrance peered at her, his eyes begging her to make some sense of what she was saying. "Well," she said, sitting back down, "since you asked. You know how you like to pray so much? How you're always going to God asking Him to forgive you for your sins—although if you ask once, I can't see why you have to keep asking—but I'm getting off track. Well, I just so happened to overhear one of your down-on-your-knees sessions when I came to meet you at the church one day. I initially just stood back to give you your time with God. I never expected to hear what I heard."

Terrance's eyes got big as she detailed word for word his almost-daily prayer for forgiveness. A prayer he'd done for years. A prayer he knew God had already answered, but one he felt compelled to deliver daily nonetheless.

"And see," she said, triumphantly finishing up what she'd overheard, "I know how you would just rather die than let anyone know your little"—she paused and chuckled—"or shall I say *humongous,* secret, which would not only leave those you know and love devastated, but would change the way everyone sees their good ol' pastor."

Savannah stood again. "So, the way I see it, being with me is a small price to pay to keep your secret."

"I . . . I can't believe you would do this," he finally managed to say.

She narrowed her eyes, the smile leaving her face. "Believe it. I tried the nice, sweet girl route and all it got me was used and abused. You're just like every other man in my life, so I'm going to use you like you used me."

"Don't you feel bad about blackmailing someone into being with you?" Terrance seemed to be grasping at straws.

"Did you feel bad when you—a so-called man of the cloth—climbed into my bed? Told me you loved me? Nope, I don't feel bad at all." She strutted to the door. "In fact, I feel quite good. After all, I'm about to become first lady of Lily Grove. What's not to be happy about?" She turned around just as she reached the door. Terrance's face looked like it had lost all of its color.

"Oh, tell your little bimbo secretary today," Savannah added. "I'll be back tomorrow so we can start planning our life together."

Savannah blew him a kiss as she headed out the door.

chapter 38

Terrance was still in shock.

He'd spent the last twenty-four hours in a daze, unable to believe what was happening to him. Just to let him know she was serious, Savannah had called last night and told his answering machine good-night (because he definitely wasn't picking up the phone). She'd wished him sweet dreams, ending the message by saying, "I love you."

He was sitting at home in the dark at the time. He'd tried to turn to the Bible to find some way to help him handle the problem, but he didn't even have the strength to open it. This was his punishment for sleeping with Savannah, especially when he knew he didn't love her and there was a strong possibility that they wouldn't be together. He'd given in to lust and was now paying the ultimate price.

And poor Raquel, she would be crushed. She'd returned to the church about an hour after Savannah left, but he couldn't even bring himself to look at her. He'd feigned a stomachache and rushed out. She, too, had been calling him all night, and he couldn't take her calls either.

He'd played out all the scenarios in his head. He could tell Savannah he wasn't giving in to the blackmail. But that could mean the end of his career—shoot, the end of everything he'd worked so hard to build—because he knew she was serious on her threat to reveal his secret.

Terrance would have stayed at home this evening, but he was supposed to be delivering part two of his lesson at Wednesday-night Bible Study, and if he missed it, Raquel would definitely know something was wrong. Besides, he probably needed Bible Study tonight more than ever.

Luckily, Raquel arrived just as he was getting Bible Study started so they didn't have time to talk, but she did shoot him a concerned look. He'd mouthed, *I'll talk to you after we finish,* and she'd nodded before taking her seat.

Terrance was about midway through his lesson when he looked up at the back of the church. Savannah had swung both of the double doors open, making a grand entrance. Everyone turned toward her as Terrance fought back the sick feeling in the pit of his stomach. He hadn't even thought about her showing up here tonight. Since he hadn't been at the church all day, he'd thought that maybe he had missed her and wouldn't have to deal with her until tomorrow. He should've known better.

"A . . . And as I was saying," Terrance said, trying to refocus, "the word of God says . . ."

Terrance tried to keep talking as Savannah made her way to the front row and sat down. Several people started grumbling and throwing her nasty looks, but she didn't seem the least bit fazed. Terrance knew his aunts were furious about the dramatic entrance. They'd been in such good moods since he'd told them he and Savannah were over. In fact, they'd been on cloud nine when they learned he was spending more and more time with Raquel.

After fumbling his way through several scriptures, Terrance wrapped up the Bible Study lesson. "Well, that's our lesson for tonight. I hope you'll notate what we discussed tonight and study it some more at home."

"Amen, Pastor," Savannah said, waving a handkerchief at him. *Since when did she ever carry a handkerchief?* Terrance thought. He forced a nod, then turned to another member, who was shooting Savannah dirty looks. "Sister Stinson, can you lead us in a closing prayer?"

"I'd love to," she said, as she stood.

"You know what, Sister Stinson," Savannah said, cutting her off. "Please allow me to close out the Bible Study."

Terrance felt his heart stop. He desperately wanted to say or do something, but it was as if his body were frozen.

Sister Stinson shot Savannah a disgruntled look, but did sit back down.

"Please bow your heads," Savannah said. "Heavenly Father, we thank you for this wonderful lesson we were blessed with this evening. Continue to watch over us and guide our steps."

Terrance was praying she'd say "amen" and wrap up, but of course, luck wasn't on his side.

"And, Lord, please bless Terrance and I as we begin our new life together. I know that marriage won't be easy, but with you at the center of our relationship, we know there's nothing we can't do. These and other blessings we ask in your name, amen."

Savannah smiled as she opened her eyes and looked around the room. Raquel, Eva, Mamie, Dorothy Mae, and half the members in the room stood with their mouths gaped open.

"What did you just say?" Mamie finally managed to say.

"Oh, that God should bless us all?" Savannah asked innocently.

"Naw, the other part," Dorothy Mae snapped.

"Oh, the part about Terrance and I getting married." Savannah was all smiles as she walked forward and took her place next to Terrance by the podium. "Yes, my baby and I are tying the knot."

Everyone in the room looked at Terrance, confused. He lowered his head. Terrance couldn't even will his mouth to open. This was definitely not how he wanted to handle this, but right now, he still couldn't find his voice.

Savannah gently pushed his shoulder. "Baby, since the cat got your tongue, I guess I'll do it." She pulled Terrance closer to her. "I would like to tell each and every one of you how much I'm looking forward to working with you here at Lily Grove. As Terrance's fiancée, I want you to see me as an extension of him."

"What in the world is going on?" Mamie yelled. Several other people started talking as well.

Terrance closed his eyes and wished he were anyplace but here.

"Terrance Deshaun Ellis, what is she talking about?" Eva demanded.

Terrance opened his eyes, but still didn't respond.

"Tell them, sweetheart," Savannah urged, a triumphant smile across her face. "Tell them, or I have so much I could tell them myself," she said when he didn't respond.

Terrance glared at her, wishing at that moment he wasn't a man of God so he could choke the crap out of her right there in the pulpit.

Finally, he turned to his members. "Sa . . . Savannah and I are . . . together," he managed to say.

" 'Together'? What does that mean?" Dorothy Mae demanded.

"Yeah, Terrance," Raquel softly added. "What does that mean?"

Savannah pursed her lips and glared at Raquel. "It means, sweetheart, that you won't be spending as much time with *my* man." The smile returned to Savannah's face as she squeezed his arm. "Now that we're engaged, he won't be needing your . . . your companionship as much." Savannah stuck out her hand, displaying a small diamond ring. Several people gasped. Terrance was one of them. They'd never said anything about getting a ring. Tears welled up in Raquel's eyes.

"Is this true?" she asked, struggling to keep her voice steady.

Savannah squeezed Terrance's arm again. "Well, tell her, sweetie."

Terrance felt like someone was taking a knife and turning it around and around in his heart. Devastation was written all over Raquel's face.

"Terrance, I asked you a question," Raquel repeated. "Is it true?"

Terrance slowly nodded. He didn't want to add to her pain by prolonging this, not to mention there was no telling what Savannah might do next.

"I can't believe you," Raquel cried as she turned and fled from the sanctuary.

Several of the members had sat back down, no doubt telling themselves this drama was much better than anything they had to get home to.

"Terrance, do you want to tell us what is going on? When did this happen? I thought you two broke up." Eva tossed the questions at him.

"We decided to work it out," Savannah offered.

"I'm not talking to you," Eva snapped.

Savannah's eyebrows raised. "Now, now. We're going to be family, so we really need to get this animosity under control."

"You will never be our family," Mamie hissed.

Savannah shrugged. "Have it your way. I'll hate, and I'm sure Terrance will hate it as well, to exclude you from his life. But we're a package deal now, and if you can't accept that, oh, well."

Terrance finally got his bearings about him. He had to get out of this sanctuary, especially with the evil and ungodly thoughts that were floating around in his head. "I need to go," he muttered.

"Yes, we do need to go," Savannah repeated as she followed Terrance toward the door. "Everyone enjoy your night. My fiancé is very tired and I want to get him home to bed."

"Terrance, you're not going anywhere!" Eva yelled. "Not until you tell us what is going on."

Terrance stopped, turned around, and looked pleadingly at his aunts. "Look, everything Savannah said is true. We're together now. Can we leave it at that? I'll talk to you all later, okay?" His head was pounding. His heart was hurting after seeing the pain in Raquel's eyes. And he wanted nothing more than to get out of the church.

"Good-bye, ladies," Savannah said. "Or shall I say, good-bye, aunties." She was on top of the world as she floated out after her fiancé.

chapter 39

Day seven of Savannah, and Terrance was going out of his mind. He had tried to go into hiding, avoiding his aunts and everyone else by saying he was sick. It wasn't a total lie. He was sick to his stomach at the thought of being blackmailed into a relationship.

And Savannah couldn't care less. She had all but moved into his place and had literally taken over his life. She talked like she wasn't blackmailing him at all.

"So, sweetie, what would you like for dinner?" she asked him this morning. "I have a beauty shop appointment, then I'm going to the grocery store. I want to make you a special dinner."

He'd done what he'd been doing for the past week: glared at her, then fell back into bed. She'd shrugged and left.

That was two hours ago. Terrance suspected she'd be returning soon, and he wasn't in the mood to deal with her happy attitude, like they were blissful newlyweds or something.

He threw back the covers, climbed out of bed, and hopped in the shower. After a ten-minute, scalding-hot shower, he felt a little better. He hurriedly got dressed and headed out before Savannah returned.

Fifteen minutes later he was parked outside the church. He sat in his car, said a brief prayer, then tried to get up the nerve to go inside. He had to snap out of this daze. Yes, his life had totally been screwed up. But he'd made this bed. It was time to lie in it. And there was no sense in his walking around moping about it.

Terrance slowly made his way in the back door and down the hall to his office. He was relieved to see that Raquel wasn't at her desk. He wasn't ready to face her, but he knew at some point he was going to have to tell her something.

Terrance wasn't in his office five minutes when there was a light tap on his door. He took a deep breath, then replied, "Come in."

"Afternoon, Pastor." Deacon Tisdale stuck his head in the door. "I saw you come in and, well, just wondered if you had a minute?"

Terrance nodded at the man, who was old enough to be his grandfather. "Sure, come on in and have a seat."

Deacon Tisdale walked in, followed by Carl Baker and Phil Wilson. Terrance forced a smile as he noticed the extreme look of concern on all of their faces.

"Gentlemen, what can I do for you?"

"Well," Deacon Tisdale began, "we know you been a little under the weather, and we wanted to see how you were doing."

Terrance nodded. "I'm doing much better, but I know you three aren't all in my office for a welfare check."

Carl stepped forward. "Actually, we're here to try and find out what's going on. You're not really engaged to that Savannah woman, are you?"

Terrance knew he owed them, as the church elders, some type of explanation. But he definitely couldn't tell them the truth.

"Well, Brother Baker, I understand you were the main one questioning my manhood," Terrance tried to joke. "Because I didn't have a woman, you didn't know if I was the right man to lead the church. In fact, didn't all of you suggest that I might need to be replaced if I didn't find a woman soon?"

None of the three men responded.

"Now that I've found a woman, seems to me you got what you wanted."

"Yeah, we wanted a first lady," Deacon Tisdale said, his voice hurried. "But not Miss Savannah."

"Do you know we'd be the laughingstock of the Baptist Association if she became our first lady?" Phil added.

"Come on, now, she's not that bad," Terrance said. *She really is,* he wanted to say, but of course he couldn't.

"I don't mean to disrespect your woman, Pastor, but everybody in town knows she's a little loose," Deacon Tisdale remarked.

"A little?" Carl retorted. He personally knew three men who had been with her, two of them within days of one another.

"She done been with half the male congregation," Phil added. Sure, he was exaggerating a bit, but in his mind, if it was more than two men, it was the same thing.

Deacon Tisdale shot Phil a menacing look. They'd

agreed not to come in and outright attack Savannah. They just wanted to gently remind Terrance about her storied reputation.

Terrance didn't really feel like coming to Savannah's defense, but if this thing with her was going to work, he had to shut down all of this negativity. "Look, Matthew, chapter seven, says, 'Judge not, lest ye be judged.' None of us are any better than anyone else. And that includes Savannah."

Deacon Tisdale was just about to say something else when Terrance's door flew open.

"Terrance Deshaun Ellis, have you lost your mind?" Eva bellowed. "You been avoiding us all week, and that hussy you call yourself engaged to wouldn't even open the door and let us in to check on you. All up in your house like she already live there. I swear to God if I wasn't saved . . ." Eva gritted her teeth as she shook her fist.

Terrance rubbed his head in exasperation. All three of his aunts stood in his doorway, looking like a pack of angry wolves. Terrance forced a smile. They obviously didn't see anything worth smiling about, because they all stood glaring at him with scowls.

"Did you have an alarm go off or something to let you know when I arrived at the office?" Terrance joked, trying to ease the tension.

"I ain't here to play with you, funny man," Eva said. "I'm here for some answers." She glared at Phil and Deacon Tisdale, who were sitting in the chairs in front of Terrance's desk. They quickly gave up their seats. "And we aren't leaving until we get those answers," Eva said, sitting down in one of the chairs. Mamie took the other.

"Yeah," Mamie added. "You got some serious explaining to do. Did you know Raquel quit? You done broke that child's heart and run her off from the church."

Terrance's heart dropped. That was the last thing he wanted.

"Now, you tell us that you had a bad reaction to some food and were delirious or something when you agreed to be with that she-devil," Eva demanded.

Terrance swallowed as his mind replayed Savannah's threat. *You'd better act like you love me or I'll tell them everything.*

"Terrance," Dorothy Mae prodded. "Please tell us this is not real."

Terrance leaned back in his chair. *I'll tell them everything,* Savannah sang in his head. "It's real, Aunt Dorothy Mae. I wish everyone around here would accept that."

It seemed everyone in the room groaned at the same time.

"I'm sorry if you all don't like Savannah, but I'm doing what's best for me." He hoped his lie was convincing because he definitely didn't feel convinced.

Eva eyed him suspiciously before saying, "So you mean to tell me you honestly think she is the lady to lead this church?"

"She may need a little work, but she has great potential. And she wants to be accepted so bad. But the bottom line is . . . I . . . she's the one I choose to be with."

No one in the room looked like they were buying his declaration.

"I will ask each of you, out of love for me, please try

to respect my decision, and my"—Terrance struggled to get the word out—"and my fiancée. This discussion is finished," he firmly said. "Now, if you all will excuse me, I have a week's worth of work to catch up on."

He buried his head back in his work, hoping they'd get the message and leave. He sighed with relief as they all left the room. But something told him their fight was far from over.

chapter 40

She has surely lost her mind. That's all Eva could think of as she watched Savannah as she all but took over the committee meeting for the Christmas celebration, which was all set to take place the Sunday before Christmas.

". . . And I really don't think the choir should wear those old stuffy, ugly blue robes. I would like to see them wear blue jeans and white shirts."

Everyone in the room looked at her like, who died and made her in charge?

Eva could no longer take it. She leaned forward. "Let me get this straight. You actually think our award-winning choir should perform at the hundred-year anniversary in their street clothes?"

"Forget this," Mamie snapped, looking around the room. "First, she come up in here talking about an outsider is gonna emcee the First Ladies' Brunch. Now this? Y'all can sit in here and act like you're okay with this woman coming in here trying to change and run things. But I refuse to do it." Mamie turned her attention back to Savannah. "You can't come up in here changing stuff."

Savannah frowned in protest. "I'm about to be first lady of this church."

"About to be," Mamie challenged. "You ain't yet."

"And you never will be if I have anything to say about it," Eva mumbled, rolling her eyes.

"Ladies," Deacon Tisdale interjected. "We're getting nowhere with this bickering. Sister Savannah, I think the proper way to handle this would be to take a vote among the committee members in regards to the choir robes."

Savannah cut her eyes and turned up her lips. "Fine."

Deacon Tisdale nodded. "Good. All those in favor of the choir performing at the Christmas celebration without their choir robes, please raise your hand."

Savannah was the only one who raised her hand. The other fourteen committee members sat stoically, with the exception of Dorothy Mae and Mamie, who had smiles across their faces.

"You know what? Whatever," Savannah said, throwing up her hands in defeat. "It's not that big of a deal anyway." She leaned back in her chair, and suddenly a smile crossed her face as her eyes lit up. "Besides, I should be leaving the celebration planning to you guys since I need to be planning the matrimonial part."

"Excuse me?" Eva said.

"Oh, Terrance didn't tell you?" Savannah said, knowing he hadn't since she'd just now come up with the idea. "Terrance and I will be getting married as part of the celebration."

"What?" several people exclaimed.

Savannah flashed a satisfied smile. "Yes, we thought that would be the perfect time to pledge our love for one another." She knew she was going a bit far, but she absolutely couldn't stand these people, and at this point she wanted to do anything to get under their skin.

"Are you out of your mind?" Eva said. "This is a highly publicized, monumental, special event to celebrate Lily Grove's one hundred years of service."

"And what better way for your pastor to celebrate than by using that opportunity to take his new wife," Savannah proclaimed.

"Sister Savannah, that's not a good idea. People are coming to help us share in our celebration, not for a wedding," Deacon Tisdale said, again trying to be the voice of reason.

"And if they care about Terrance, they won't mind taking twenty minutes out of the service to watch him marry the woman he loves."

Mamie and Dorothy Mae let out loud groans.

"That will not happen," Eva said matter-of-factly.

Savannah met her glare with just as much passion. "Yes. It will." She stood from the table. "And I'm going to go finish my planning. I have so much to do. I'll leave the rest of the celebration to you guys." Savannah made her way to the door.

She was barely out of the room before Eva turned to the rest of the committee. "This absolutely will not happen. I mean, a wedding at the Christmas celebration? That is just too much."

"So what are we gonna do?" Carl asked.

Mamie cut her eyes at him. "Shut up, Carl. This is all

your fault anyway. You were the one spearheading this whole 'Pastor needs to get a woman or go' campaign. Well, he got a woman. You happy?"

Before Carl could respond, another female committee member interjected, "We've got to do something. This was supposed to be a first-class affair. We'll be the laughingstock of the town."

"I'll figure something out," Eva responded. "Give me a day or two, but rest assured this wedding will not happen."

Eva knew trying to talk some sense into Terrance wouldn't do any good. For some reason, that girl had his nose wide-open, and Eva didn't think anything she said would get through to him. Nope, they'd have to find some other way to deal with Miss Savannah, and they had to find it quick.

chapter 41

"Girl, you are off the chain." Tyra laughed as she looked through yet another wedding catalog.

"Shoot, I told you those women didn't know who they were messing with." Savannah had come home with an armful of wedding magazines and told Tyra they needed to get into speed-planning mode. The Christmas celebration was right around the corner, and that left her with little time to get everything together.

"I'm still not understanding how you got Terrance to go for all of this," Tyra said, shaking her head.

"I told you, he knows what's best for him."

"Girl, what do you have over him? It must be major. That's the only thing I can think of as to why he'd go along with your outrageous demands."

Savannah flashed a knowing smile. "If I tell you, I'd have to kill you."

"Come on, tell me what's going on," Tyra pleaded.

"In due time, darling, in due time. Right now, just rest assured that Terrance may have reluctantly gone into this relationship, but before all is said and done, he'll be madly in love with me."

Tyra shook her head again. "Girl, you're delusional."

"Nope, just confident. He's still a little angry that I'm forcing him right now, but he's coming around. I think he's warming to the idea."

"What happened to that secretary?"

"I don't know and I don't care." Savannah paused and pointed at a dress in *Brides* magazine. "Oooh, I like that one. I hope they have it in stock because I don't have time to order anything."

Tyra nodded her approval.

"Anyway," Savannah continued, "I heard she quit. I haven't seen her at church lately, so hopefully she transferred churches, too."

"Are you inviting your mom?"

"Please. That old drunk isn't coming anywhere near my wedding. She'd find some way to ruin it. It's bad enough my grandmother will be there—probably in a hoochie leather dress." Savannah snorted.

"Well, are you going to have attendants and stuff?"

"Only you—that is, if you're willing," Savannah said sweetly.

"Girl, who are you kidding. I told you, I wouldn't miss that day for nothing in the world."

"Awww, that's so sweet. I'm so happy it means that much to you."

"Girl, I wouldn't miss it because all hell is gon' break loose in the church house that day." Tyra laughed as Savannah threw a pillow at her.

They flipped through several more magazines and

catalogs. Finally, after about an hour, Tyra said, "I'm beat. I think you should go with that first dress you found and call it a day."

Savannah had actually stopped looking through the magazines and was staring out into space. Tyra noticed the change in her demeanor.

"Hey, are you all right?" Tyra asked, sitting up.

"Huh?" Savannah said, snapping out of her thoughts.

"I said, are you all right? You seemed like you were in another place."

Savannah let out a long sigh as she closed the magazine and leaned back on the sofa herself. "I'm okay. Just a little tired I guess."

Tyra stared at her friend. She'd known Savannah for almost ten years and could tell when something was bothering her.

"Can I ask you a question?"

"Shoot," Savannah said as she massaged her forehead.

"Are you sure you're doing the right thing? I mean, making Terrance marry you and all?"

Savannah didn't look at Tyra.

"I mean, I'm not trying to piss you off or nothing," Tyra continued, "but I just know that deep down, you wanted things to be different."

Savannah let out a heavy sigh. "I did want them to be different. But they aren't. I wanted Terrance to love me, and I think he could have. I wish I could erase my past, but I can't. I made a lot of mistakes, did some stupid things, but it's not right for people to stand in judgment of me all the time. I don't have anyone on my side in that church."

"I'm on your side." Tyra smiled widely.

Savannah returned the grin. "I know, but you don't ever come to church."

Tyra took a deep breath. "Okay, okay, as your best friend, when you become first lady, I'll come to church more often."

Savannah tried to laugh as she shook her head. "Why won't these people give me a chance?" she said, her laughter dying down.

"Maybe because you're being just as nasty to them as they are to you," Tyra replied matter-of-factly.

"But I tried to be nice. No one accepted that. And I'm not just gon' let them talk to me any kind of way and treat me like crap."

"I'm not saying you should, but my grandma always used to say you get more flies with sugar than sh—"

"There you go with your grandma's cockamamy sayings," Savannah said, cutting her off. "I feel you, though. I'm going to have to do something, because I don't want to spend the rest of my life in a constant battle with the people at church."

Tyra shuddered. "Ughhh, the rest of your life. You really think you'll be married that long?"

"Tyra, I'm serious, Terrance is my soul mate. When I marry him, I want that to be it. I'm going to be a loving, faithful wife that gives my man everything he wants and needs."

Tyra turned up her nose. "More power to you. Ugghhh. Forever is a mighty long time."

Savannah glanced down at the dress she was most likely going to choose. "And it's the only way I want it. I just hope I can get Terrance to agree."

chapter 42

The sickness wasn't going away. Terrance hadn't felt right since Savannah had demanded that he marry her. And things had just gotten worse when she demanded it take place at the Christmas celebration. He felt like he was just existing. He knew things were bad because he couldn't even find solace in the Word, and that's something that seldom happened.

The only good thing to come out of all this was that Savannah had been so engrossed in wedding plans that she was staying out of his hair.

His aunts had all but disowned him, even missing church the last few Sundays out of protest. And to make matters worse, he still hadn't made amends with Raquel. He'd finally broken down and tried to call her, but she never took his calls, nor did she ever call him back.

Terrance unlocked the door to the church. He was grateful that the building was empty as he really wasn't up to dealing with anyone.

He had just walked into his office when he noticed her.

"Raquel?" She was at her desk outside his office.

He'd obviously startled her because she jumped. "Oh, I'm sorry. I didn't think you'd be here. You had a barbershop appointment today."

"They were crowded and I didn't think I'd make it out in time to be back before Bible Study." Terrance stared at her, taking in her beauty. She had her hair down and looked gorgeous in a brown velour warm-up. "No, I'm . . . I'm happy to see you." Why had he not tried to pursue her a long time ago? She was everything he ever wanted in a woman. Maybe if he hadn't been trying to be so respectful of her relationship with Dolan, they'd be together and he wouldn't be in this mess with Savannah.

Raquel finished putting some things in a box. "I just stopped by to get the rest of the things from my desk. And to drop off the keys. Sorry it took so long but . . ." She didn't finish her sentence, instead letting her words trail off as she looked away.

"I didn't see your car," Terrance said, struggling for conversation.

"I parked on the other side of the church because I didn't know you'd fixed the door back here."

An awkward silence briefly hung between them. "Well, I better get going," she finally said, walking from the back of her desk.

Terrance stepped in front of her. "Why did you quit?"

She looked at him, and he could see the tears forming in her eyes. "Why do you think?" she gently replied.

"Raquel, please let me explain."

"There's nothing to explain, Terrance. You made your decision."

"It's not like that at all."

"I heard you were getting married at the Christmas celebration. Is that true?"

Terrance diverted his eyes.

Raquel let out a pained laugh. "Leave it to Savannah to try and show up the church." Raquel tried again to step around him. "I hope you and Savannah are very happy."

Terrance grabbed her arm. "Please. I never meant to hurt you."

Raquel stopped, took a deep breath, then looked him directly in the eyes. "I would hate to see the pain you could cause if you ever did mean to hurt me."

Her words stung. Terrance found himself fighting back tears himself. He'd never realized just how deeply he cared for Raquel until this very moment. "I love you, Raquel." He knew he shouldn't go there, but it was as if his heart took on a voice of its own.

Tears slowly began streaming down Raquel's face. "How can you stand there and say that to me?"

"Because it's true."

She wiped her eyes, like she was determined not to cry. "If it was, you wouldn't be about to marry another woman."

"I told you it wasn't like that."

Raquel set the box down. "Then what is it like, Terrance? Help me out here, because I'm not understanding. One minute you're professing your love for me, telling me how much you want me. The next minute you're engaged to the woman you led me to believe you couldn't stand."

"I never said I couldn't stand her."

Raquel threw up her hands. "Gimme a break, Terrance. You know what you did." She reached for her box. He stopped her.

"I don't love Savannah."

Raquel glared at him, obviously trying to gauge whether he was telling her the truth. "Then why are you marrying her? You found out she was really pregnant? Help me understand."

Terrance rubbed his hand over his face. "Have a seat." Raquel didn't move. "Please? I'll explain everything."

Raquel sat down in the wingback chair in the lobby of Terrance's office suite.

"I'm listening."

"I don't know how to say this," he began as he sat down next to her. "But long story short, Savannah is blackmailing me into marrying her."

Terrance didn't know how much he planned to tell Raquel. Part of him just wanted to share his dilemma with someone. The other part felt he owed her the truth.

"Blackmail?" Raquel asked incredulously.

Terrance nodded.

"Oh my God. What could she possibly have on you?"

"It's just so hard," he groaned. "If I tell you, it might change the way you look at me."

Raquel took his hand. "Terrance, I love you. Everything about you." She stroked his face. "There is nothing you can say or do that will change that."

Lord, please guide me right now, Terrance silently prayed. Suddenly, as if God Himself had whispered the answer in his ear, Terrance began sharing his story.

chapter 43

Raquel sat at a loss for words. Her heart ached as she imagined Terrance carrying around that secret for so long. Then she felt her anger building at the thought that Savannah was actually using that information to make him marry her!

"Terrance, I am so sorry," Raquel finally said, as she wiped away the single tear trickling down his cheek.

"It's nothing for you to be sorry about."

"But the guilt. I know it's been eating you alive."

Terrance nodded. "It has. And because I never faced it, I'm now paying for it."

"Terrance, I know this is pretty bad, but marrying Savannah is not the answer." Raquel took his hands.

Terrance leaned back in his chair. "Then what is? Come clean and break everyone's heart, not to mention—"

"Oh, I don't think so!" Savannah's boisterous voice cut him off.

Terrance looked up to his doorway to see Savannah wiggling her neck, about to go ballistic.

"I know you're not sitting up in here holding hands with her, all deep in some conversation!"

Terrance glanced down. He hadn't even realized Raquel was still holding his hands. He eased them away.

"Savannah," Terrance said. "It's not what it looks like."

"Don't 'Savannah' me," she said, stomping into his office. "What exactly are you doing up in here with her?"

Raquel stood, looking extremely uneasy. "I just came to get the rest of my things."

"Well, get them and go, tramp!" Savannah snapped.

"Look here," Raquel said, taking a step toward Savannah.

Terrance stepped in before Raquel could say anything. "Savannah, enough. That is totally uncalled for."

"I'll tell you what's uncalled for," Savannah began.

But before she could continue, Eva appeared in the doorway. "Good Lord Almighty, what's all this ruckus in here?" Her eyes danced back and forth between Terrance, Raquel, and Savannah.

"Hi, Miss Eva," Raquel said. "I just came to get the last of my things. I was just leaving."

"You doggone right you leaving," Savannah yelled. "I'm sick of all y'all. Go back to your fiancé and let him beat your ass some more, I don't care, just stay away from Terrance."

Eva's mouth dropped open, as did those of a few other people who had begun to gather outside Terrance's office.

"Cuz if your little yellow behind comes sniffing around my man anymore, it's gon' be on!" Savannah continued her rampage. Raquel glared at her like she wanted to claw her eyes out with her bare hands.

"Oh, my God," Eva muttered, clutching the cross around her neck.

Terrance grabbed Savannah's arm and pushed her back against the wall. He definitely hadn't meant to manhandle her, but she was out of control. "You need to calm down!" he yelled.

"I know you didn't just put your hands on me! You think I'm playing with you?" she shouted. Terrance had lost his mind. First, he was sneaking off with that hussy Raquel, now he had the nerve to push her! "Do you think I'm playing with you?" She looked at Eva. "You wanna know all about your perfect little angel here?"

Raquel immediately stepped in. "Savannah, I'm leaving, okay? I won't be back, so you don't have to worry about me anymore. Just please calm down. There was nothing going on. I was just saying good-bye. You and Terrance are about to be married. Don't do anything you might regret," Raquel calmly warned.

Savannah eyed Raquel suspiciously, but she did settle down. She couldn't believe she'd gone off like that and was about to blow everything before they even said "I do." But seeing the two of them together just made her snap.

Terrance was standing next to Savannah; the color seemed to have drained from his face.

"Ms. Eva," Raquel said, turning to her, "you take care of yourself."

Eva was still too stunned to reply. Raquel picked up her box, made her way through the small crowd, and left.

"I do not believe you did that," Terrance hissed, finally finding his voice.

Savannah flung her hair out of her face and tried to

stand up straight. "Believe it. And let the witch show up here again, and it's going to be even worse. Now, I'm going to the sanctuary to wait on Bible Study to begin. I'm feeling like I need the Word today." Then Savannah sashayed out past everyone, like she didn't have a care in the world.

Eva slammed the door. She didn't want the nosy church members all in their conversation. She spun on Terrance. "And you're telling me that's what you want in a wife? In a first lady?" she asked, dumbfounded.

Terrance closed his eyes and sighed. "Please, Aunt Eva, don't start."

"I'm just trying to get you to be reasonable. Ain't no sex that good where you should be willing to put up with that nonsense."

He opened his eyes and stared at his aunt. "What in the world are you talking about?"

"Sex. She's whippin' it on you real good. That can be the only possible reason why you would choose a woman like her over someone like Raquel." Eva crossed her arms under her chest like she had figured it all out.

Terrance contemplated replying, then decided against it. "Just leave me alone. I wish everyone would just leave me alone." Terrance grabbed his keys and stormed toward the door. "Can you ask Reverend Gibson to conduct Bible Study? I need to leave."

"Terrance!" Eva called out after him. "Don't you walk away from me!"

Terrance ignored her cries as he bolted out of his office, past the few onlookers still gathered outside in the hallway, and out to his car. His life was spiraling out of control and he didn't know how much more of this he could take.

chapter 44

"So are you still mad at me?" Savannah poked her head in Terrance's bedroom. He rolled his eyes as he lay across his bed, his unopened Bible in front of him.

He'd heard her come in, with the key she'd conveniently made for herself shortly after their "engagement." She was taking over his life and there wasn't a doggone thing he could do about it.

"I'm really sorry, baby," Savannah said as she sat down on the bed next to him. He didn't turn over as she began softly stroking the back of his head. "I know you're mad, but I just kind of flipped out when I saw you sitting there holding Raquel's hand. I know how bad she wants you."

I want her, too, Terrance wanted to scream.

"Baby." Savannah's voice was laced with sweetness. It made Terrance want to throw up. "I know you don't understand or agree with what I'm doing, but I think if you just open up your heart, you'll see that I'm doing the right thing for us."

"How is this right for us, Savannah?" Terrance said, finally turning over. She had the nerve to actually have tears in her eyes. He wasn't moved. He couldn't be. Not with everything she was putting him through.

"Terrance, I love you with all my heart. I just want you to love me, too," she whispered.

"And you think this is the way to make that happen?" he asked, sitting up.

Savannah lowered her head and started toying with the scarf belt wrapped around her waist. "I tried the right way and it got me nowhere."

"No, your lying and deceitfulness got you nowhere."

A tear fell from the corner of her eye. "You act like you've never done anything that you needed to be forgiven for. And we both know that's not the case."

Terrance stared at her. That hurt. But he guessed that she meant for it to. He let out a dejected sigh. Maybe if he tried to reason with her, talk to her from a spiritual perspective and not with all the hostility he'd had since she'd dropped this bombshell on him, he could make more progress. "Trust me, Savannah, I've done my fair share of sinning, but I pray that God will continue to direct my path so that I can live my life as a blessing to Him. It's one thing when we mess up, but it's when we continue to do wrong, when we know it's wrong, that things become problematic."

Savannah looked away, and Terrance reached out to take her hand.

"And this, trying to blackmail me into marriage, is wrong."

Savannah snatched her hand away. He was getting to her for a minute, but she shook off any remorse that may have been creeping into her heart. "Whatever, Terrance. God talks to me, too, you know. And He told me that you were my soul mate, even if you don't believe it. And I'm going to do whatever I have to do so that we end up together because I'm confident that eventually, you'll come around."

This woman can't possibly be serious, Terrance thought. "Savannah, listen to what you're saying."

Savannah stood up. "I'm making lasagna for dinner. Do you want a Caesar or traditional salad with that?"

"Can we finish this?"

"It's finished," Savannah replied, walking to the door. "The Christmas celebration and our wedding is in three days. The brunch is the day after tomorrow. We have a lot to do and we don't need to sit around talking about things that won't change. I still need to pack all my stuff. The movers will be bringing my things over the day after our wedding. You know in our haste, we didn't talk about where we're going for our honeymoon. Oh, well, I'll think of something. We'll probably just have to do something small now, and you can take me on a tropical vacation later, when you're deeply in love with me," Savannah rambled. "I love you and I'm going to make dinner, then I'll make sure everything is good to go for what I'm sure will be the happiest day of my life."

She flashed a smile before leaving the room.

chapter 45

Eva stared at the hot wings in disgust. Mamie walked up to her. She must've been reading Eva's mind because she said, "I can't believe she ordered hot wings. It's a brunch, for Christ's sake."

Eva massaged her temples. "And they're from Hooters at that." Eva pointed to the platter that had the word *Hooters* etched across the plastic cover.

"She could've had the decency to put them in a nice plate or something," Dorothy Mae added as she joined her sisters at the hors d'oeuvres table. They were the first to arrive at the brunch, besides Savannah. Dorothy Mae and Mamie almost didn't come out of protest, but Eva had convinced them that they needed to be there.

Mamie rolled her eyes. "Is this what we have to look forward to?"

"The first ladies and other guests will begin arriving any minute now," Eva said as she began gathering up the wing platter. "And I refuse to be the laughingstock of the entire city when they walk up in here and see some dag-gone hot wings."

"Umm, excuse me, where are you going with that?" Savannah asked, walking up just as Eva had picked up the platter.

"I'm taking it to the back," Eva said defiantly. "We will not serve hot wings at this event."

"Last time I checked, I was hosting this shindig." Savannah placed her hands on her hips. Eva's eyes roamed Savannah's body. She had on a fur stole, a cream satiny blouse, and a leather skirt. Thank God the skirt at least came to her knees.

"You do realize it's sixty-five degrees outside," Dorothy Mae said, eyeing Savannah as well.

"It's still winter," Savannah snapped, fingering her stole. "As I said"—she turned back to Eva— "this is my event, and I want hot wings."

"This is a brunch, Savannah!" Eva was trying not to lose her cool.

"I know that, and I have Mrs. Williams bringing some grits."

Eva pursed her lips. She couldn't believe Sister Williams hadn't warned her about this foolishness.

"Grits? And hot wings?" Eva said through clenched teeth.

"If you got out of your small little world sometimes, you'd know that grits and chicken wings are a delicacy on the West Coast," Savannah replied as she reached for the tray.

"Well, we ain't on the West Coast," Eva said, pulling the tray out of her reach. "And in the South we don't eat Hooters' hot wings for brunch."

Dorothy Mae tugged at Eva's arm just as two women walked into the room.

"Go greet your guests," Eva said as she quickly turned and walked back to the kitchen. If they had to have the wings, she was at least going to put them on a decorative plate.

Savannah fought back the anger that was building inside her. She was not going to let them, or anyone for that matter, ruin her first chance to show these people she was worthy of being a first lady.

"Good morning, ladies," Savannah said, spinning around to greet the two women. "I'm Sister Savannah McKinney, soon to be first lady of Lily Grove." She reached over and hugged both women. "Thank you so much for coming. And you are?"

Both women flashed genuine smiles as they introduced themselves. Savannah walked them over to one of the brunch volunteers, who helped them to their seats.

As Savannah began greeting more guests, Eva returned with the wings on a platter. "Umph, she sure is putting on a show, huh?" Eva said as she set the wings on the table.

Mamie frowned in disgust. "Walking around like she been a first lady for ten years or something."

"The visitors sho' do seem to take a likin' to her though," Dorothy Mae said as they watched Savannah laugh with the first lady from New Jeremiah.

"That's cuz they don't know her," Mamie snarled.

"Well, regardless, we need to put on our pleasant faces," Eva said, brushing down her skirt. "We can't let folks know about the dissension at our church."

Eva walked over and began mingling with some of the guests, who had quickly begun arriving. Her sisters didn't join her, but she knew it would take a minute for them to warm to the idea of Savannah hosting the event.

Savannah gave everyone time to get settled before taking the podium. She was all smiles as she welcomed everyone to what would be "the first of many events" she would be hosting as first lady.

"And I am so excited that most of you will be there to share in my joy tomorrow as I wed the man of my dreams," Savannah announced.

Mamie coughed loudly, then looked down and began toying with her napkin as several people glanced her way. Eva shot her sister the evil eye to get her to straighten up.

Savannah ignored Mamie's coughing fit and continued, "At this time, I will turn our program over to your mistress of ceremonies for today, Sister Rachel Jackson Adams from Zion Hill Baptist Church."

Eva forced a smile as she clapped along with everyone else for Rachel. She'd been against having that woman serve as mistress of ceremonies because her drama-filled past was almost as bad as Savannah's. But at least Rachel had reformed some, at least from what Eva had heard. And as Rachel took the podium, she actually wore a look of confidence and exuded the demeanor of a proper first lady, something Eva didn't think Savannah would ever be capable of.

Savannah took her seat at the head table. She was proud of how things were going so far. As she watched Sister Adams flawlessly navigate the program, she was happy that she'd stood her ground on having Rachel emcee. Savannah had only met her a couple of times, but she felt like she could relate to Rachel because she had been unwanted in her church as well. But now, her members loved her. That's what Savannah was hoping would happen with her. But what Savannah liked most was that Rachel seemed to keep it real, no matter whom she was dealing with. That's the type of first lady Savannah planned to be.

The two-hour program was over before Savannah knew it. The guest speaker, Evangelist Jocelyn Rogers, was phenomenal, and everyone had sung her praises after it was over. A few people from Lily Grove, including Terrance's aunts, refused to give Savannah any props, but they didn't have to. She knew she had done an excellent job, especially with such short planning time.

"So, Ms. Eva, the people really seemed to enjoy the hot wings," a satisfied Savannah said.

"Church folks are usually nice—in your face. Then talk about you behind your back," Eva snidely remarked. "So I wouldn't read too much into it."

Savannah contemplated coming back with a retort of her own, but she was tired of the attitudes, the wall she had built. She sighed and said, "Ms. Eva, can we please go over here and talk for a minute." Savannah pointed at a corner table.

Eva glanced over at her sisters, who were talking to one of the guests that was still hanging around. She turned her attention back to Savannah. The sincere look on Savannah's face caused Eva to let down her guard just a little bit. "Fine," she said as she walked to the table.

"I know I've done some things you don't approve of," Savannah said after they were both seated at the table.

"Some?"

"Please let me finish." Savannah inhaled, trying to tell herself not to go off, no matter what. "But I just wish you'd give me a chance. I really am a good person, and if all of you would just give me a chance to show you, I think you'd see that."

Eva softened her expression and pointedly asked, "Why are you marrying my nephew?"

Savannah stared directly in Eva's eyes. "Because I love him more than I've ever loved any man in my life."

Savannah took a deep breath, then continued, "You don't have to respond right now. Just please think about burying the hatchet. All I want to do is make Terrance happy. Something we both want." She stood up. "He and I are getting married tomorrow, and the best gift we can give Terrance is to find a way to get along."

Savannah gave one last pleading look before walking away from the table. She silently prayed that Tyra was right. She hoped she could get a lot further by being nice.

chapter 46

Terrance seemed to be just going through the motions. Every fiber of his being was telling him to march out into that sanctuary and tell everyone his secret, then tell Savannah where she could go. But when he thought of his aunts—and all the other people who would be disappointed—he just couldn't bring himself to do it.

"This is my punishment," he mumbled as he adjusted his tie. He stared at himself in the full-length mirror in the corner of his office. Never in a million years did he think his wedding day would be like this. He was here physically, but mentally, his mind was anywhere but here. Terrance had to say a quick prayer of forgiveness when he found himself wishing Savannah would get hit by a truck or something on her way to the church.

"Knock, knock," Monty said, pushing the office door open.

"What's up, man?" Terrance asked, turning to his friend. Monty looked quite nice in his double-breasted suit. Neither of them had bothered with a tux. "I'm glad you came."

"You know I wouldn't miss this for the world. You know how I feel about you marrying this chick, but I'm here to support you. If this is what you really want to do, then I'm with you."

"Thanks, man. I really appreciate that."

"This *is* really what you want to do?" Monty asked suspiciously.

Terrance forced a smile. He wanted to tell Monty the truth, but he just knew Monty would tell him not to marry Savannah, and Terrance just didn't need that stress right now.

"Are there any people here yet?"

"Yeah, a few. I'm glad you at least got Savannah to have the wedding right before the Christmas celebration."

"Yeah, because she definitely was trying to have it right smack-dab in the middle of the service." Terrance stopped and stared at Monty, who was looking around nervously. "Why are you looking like that?"

"Oh, umm," Monty said, raising his eyebrows. "Th . . . There's someone that wants to holla at you real quick."

"Who?" Terrance said, glancing toward the door.

"The woman you should be marrying," Monty said matter-of-factly.

Terrance's eyes lit up. "Raquel is here?"

"Yeah. She cornered me in the hallway and told me to come see if you were alone. She's hiding around the corner and stuff like she's James Bond."

"Go get her," Terrance excitedly said. "Tell her she can come in."

Monty chuckled. "I figured you would say that. I'll be right back."

"And, Monty," Terrance said, stopping him at the door.

"Yeah?"

"Can you keep an eye out for Savannah and make sure she doesn't come back here?"

Monty nodded. "You ain't said nothing but a word." Monty poked his head out the door and motioned down the hallway. A few seconds later, Raquel eased into Terrance's office. Monty quickly excused himself. Terrance felt himself relax.

"Hey," Raquel said.

"Hey," Terrance replied. They stood in awkward silence for a few minutes.

"I hope you don't mind that I came," Raquel finally said.

"You know I don't." Terrance took in her beauty. As usual, she was a vision of loveliness in a beige, fitted, knee-length dress and brown boots. "Although, I'm surprised that you're here."

Raquel glanced down. "I wasn't going to come, but I had to try one more time to convince you that you don't have to do this."

Images of Savannah spilling his secret to anyone who would listen flashed through his head. At the same time, images of the life he wanted with Raquel began to overshadow thoughts of Savannah.

"I love you so much." Terrance exhaled as he stepped toward Raquel.

She closed her eyes and inhaled. When she opened them, a tear had begun to form in the corner of her eye. "Then don't do this. I love you, too. This is killing me. You don't have to do this. I will stand by you to the end," she said, her voice cracking.

Terrance reached out and took her in his arms. He was confused. As he hugged her, everything felt so right. He squeezed her harder, wishing they could just disappear. He had just buried his nose in her hair, inhaling her scent, when a loud ruckus brought him back to reality.

"I don't care who you are, you're not going in there!" Terrance heard Monty scream.

Terrance groaned. Savannah must have come to his chambers and was now outside acting a fool.

Terrance pulled himself away and was just about to say something to Raquel when his door burst open, slamming against the wall and knocking the pictures to the floor.

"Wha—?" Terrance exclaimed.

"See, I knew I wasn't no fool!"

Raquel's eyes grew wide. "Dolan!"

"Don't Dolan me, you cheating piece of trash!" He angrily stepped toward Raquel. Monty was right behind him, his suit messed up like he'd been tussling with Dolan, which Terrance had no doubt that he had.

Terrance quickly jumped in front of Raquel, shielding her from Dolan's wrath.

Dolan stopped, took a deep breath, and pursed his lips. "Dude, if you know what's best for you, you will get out of my face."

Monty looked like he was about to rush Dolan, but Terrance held up his hand to keep Monty back.

"No, brother, I think it's you who needs to get out of my office and out of my church."

Dolan suddenly burst out laughing. Everyone stared at him strangely as he doubled over. "Y'all think this is some kind of joke." He laughed before reaching in his jacket and pulling out a small, chrome pistol. He stood back and pointed the gun at Terrance's head. "Do I look like a comedian?"

Raquel screamed as Terrance tensed up. Dolan quickly pointed the gun at Monty, who looked like he was ready to pounce.

"Make a move, punk, and it will be your last," Dolan warned.

Monty backed down, his teeth gritted. "Let's see how bad you are without the gun, bruh."

Dolan scratched his head with the barrel of the gun. "Ummm, let me ponder that. Now why would I want to do something like that? Cuz this here"—he waved the gun around—"says that I'm in control." He pointed the gun back at Monty. "Now get out."

"I ain't goin' nowhere," Monty shot back.

"Fool, did that sound like a request?" Dolan moved the gun closer to Monty's head.

"Monty, go on. Leave," Terrance gently said. "We'll be okay."

"Yeah, Monty, go on and leave. Before the good reverend has to clean your blood up off his plush carpet here."

Monty glared at Dolan as he made his way to the door. Terrance tried to give him a reassuring look, even though he was scared out of his mind.

"Dolan, please don't do this," Raquel tearfully pleaded

as soon as Monty was out the door. "I'll go with you, just please don't do this."

Dolan turned the gun back on Terrance. "I have a good mind to just blast this fool right here so I don't have to worry about his sanctified ass no more."

Raquel tried to step out from behind Terrance. "Please, I'm sorry. Let's just leave."

Terrance tried to grab Raquel's arm. "No!"

Dolan grabbed Raquel's other arm as he aimed the gun right between Terrance's eyes. "I don't have no problem with shooting a man of God right here in church."

Terrance backed down. He couldn't believe this madman was about to take the woman he loved and do God only knew what to her, and he felt helpless to stop him.

Just then, Terrance's office door swung open again. This time it was Savannah, standing there in her white Vera Wang wedding gown. "What in the world is going on? Monty is yelling for someone to call the cops—" Savannah stopped talking when she noticed Dolan with his arm around Raquel's neck, the gun now pointed at her head.

"Oh, my God," Savannah mumbled.

"Move out the way!" Dolan yelled at Savannah as he pulled Raquel toward the door.

Savannah ran over and ducked behind Terrance, who still stood defensively, contemplating whether he should try to take Dolan.

Savannah must have read his mind because she whispered, "Let them go, baby. This isn't your battle."

Dolan looked crazed as he dragged Raquel out into the hallway. "Say good-bye to your little boyfriend," he growled. "You thought I was playing when I told you if I couldn't have you, no one would?"

Dolan kicked open the sanctuary door and dragged Raquel down the aisle to the altar. The few people who had already arrived screamed as they scattered. Some ducked behind the pews, others ran out of the building.

"Till death do us part, baby!" Dolan yelled as he pushed Raquel down on the floor in front of the pulpit. "That was supposed to be our vow to each other, right? Till death do us part."

Terrance, Savannah, Monty, and several other people stood helplessly at the back of the church as Raquel continued to sob. Dolan cocked the gun, then pointed it at her heart.

Then, the only sound in the sanctuary was a hail of gunfire as Terrance felt his whole world go black.

chapter 47

"This is supposed to be my wedding day!" Savannah cried. "Why did they have to ruin my wedding day?"

Terrance looked at Savannah with utter disgust as he watched her stomp across the hospital waiting room, her train draped up in her arms. He couldn't believe that was all she cared about.

"Why they had to choose my wedding day, and my wedding, to do this is beyond me!" she ranted.

"Savannah, shut up and sit down!" Terrance snapped. She had been going on nonstop since they'd left the church.

Savannah glared at him. "You heard the doctor say she's going to be fine. He shot her in the freaking arm! The doctor said she can probably go home tomorrow."

Terrance was so upset he couldn't even respond.

"I don't understand why we couldn't go ahead with the wedding," Savannah continued. "Your little former secretary didn't need to be there anyway. And it's not like she died or was anywhere near death."

"She didn't die, Savannah, but Dolan did! In the exact same spot we were supposed to get married. Are you really telling me we should've just moved his body and continued with the ceremony?"

Savannah rolled her eyes. It did sound kind of stupid when he said it like that.

"I didn't mean it like that," she whined. "I was just so close to having my wildest dreams come true, and now it's all been ruined because of that maniac!"

As far as Savannah was concerned, Dolan deserved to get shot. She just wished the cops had found somewhere else to do it.

After Dolan had fired one shot at Raquel, police, who had seemingly come from nowhere, opened fire. Savannah had no idea how many rounds they fired, but it was enough to kill Dolan on the spot. Of course, Terrance had rushed right to Raquel's side. And only after she opened her eyes did he seem halfway relieved.

"Savannah, maybe it's better if you go home," Eva said, snapping Savannah out of her thoughts. Eva and her sisters had arrived at the church just as the drama was unfolding.

Savannah glared at Eva. "I'm not going anywhere. As long as Terrance is here, I'm not moving."

"It's not like you even care about Raquel," Mamie added.

"Look—," Savannah began.

"Not now! Good grief, would all of you just be quiet!" Terrance quietly screamed. He buried his face in his hands, the tears overtaking him. "I can't take this, I can't take this, I can't take this," he mumbled.

The outburst caught them all by surprise. Savannah

quietly sat down on the hard sofa next to him, mumbling a halfhearted apology.

Terrance felt like he was having a meltdown. The thought of almost losing Raquel was causing him to reevaluate everything he'd been doing.

Savannah reached over and gently placed her hand on top of his. He wanted to snatch it away, but instead he just sighed as he realized that it was time for all of this to end.

chapter 48

Terrance walked to the podium at Lily Grove. This had to have been the longest week of his life. But it felt good to be back in the pulpit. He'd turned his troubles over to God, *really* turned them over, and stopped trying to figure out the answers himself. God had revealed to him what he needed to do.

Terrance smiled at Raquel, who was sitting in the second row. He was so happy to see her here. She'd told him last night she had "to be in the house of the Lord" today.

Savannah caught Terrance looking at Raquel and turned up her nose. For one quick minute she found herself wishing Dolan had been successful in shooting Raquel. She shook off the evil thought and tried to focus her attention back on Terrance.

She had gently reminded him this morning that they still had an agreement. He would still marry her, and she would take his secret to her grave. He hadn't responded, but he hadn't fought her on it either. He'd been walking around numb all week. Savannah knew he was dealing with a lot, so she actually let him have his space. All of her attention was focused on marrying Terrance as quickly as possible.

"God always says you have to be tested to have a testimony," Terrance began. "And I think you all will agree with me when I say we all have been tested this week."

A chorus of *Amens* rang through the sanctuary.

Terrance looked down at the spot where Dolan had died. The deacons had quickly had the carpet changed, but the image remained fresh in his mind.

"I know a lot of you were upset that our Christmas celebration was marred by the events that unfolded here last week." Terrance paused as several people grumbled. "But we have to remember, that which does not break us makes us stronger. And, church, I stand before you a stronger man today."

Terrance took a deep breath as several people stood and urged him to "tell it." He looked at Raquel. Her arm was in a sling. She gave him a reassuring nod.

"I have something I need to share." Terrance turned his attention to his aunts, all of whom sat in the front row. "To my beloved aunts. You have nurtured me, raised me, and loved me. And even though I haven't always acted like it, I am and I will always be eternally grateful."

Savannah raised her eyebrows. His aunts looked at him like they were trying to figure out where he was going with his testimony.

"I have prayed about this, and there's just no other way to say what I have to say except to come right out and say it."

The entire church was quiet now.

Terrance paused and took a sip of water. "I have been carrying a secret that has all but eaten me alive."

Savannah jumped from her seat. "Terrance, no! Don't do this. Please."

Terrance looked at her pitifully. "Savannah, please sit down. It's over. There will be no wedding."

Savannah looked around at all the people staring at her, and defeat set in. She slowly sat back down, seemingly stunned that everything she had ever dreamed of was coming to an end.

Terrance took another deep breath. "Church, as many of you know, my beloved grandmother died fourteen years ago at the hands of a drunk driver. It devastated me, her sisters, and you, her church family who knew and loved her." Terrance didn't realize he was crying until he saw the tears drop on his open Bible. "Despite their best efforts, police never found that person. Despite my aunts' tireless search for exactly what happened and who caused that deadly accident, no one ever could find the person who killed my grandmother. That's because he was under their noses the whole time. I am that drunk driver. I am the person who killed my grandmother."

Eva, Mamie, and Dorothy Mae let out a collective gasp, as did several other people in the sanctuary. Terrance knew he'd lose his nerve if he didn't continue.

"Despite the love of my family, I was a misguided young man who didn't know God and turned to my friends, my so-called friends, who continued to lead me down the wrong path." He paused and wiped away his tears.

"I was in a stolen car that night. I didn't take it, but my friend did. I dropped him off at a girl's house after a night of drinking and partying. It was my intention to get home, dump the car down the street, and get some sleep. I never made it home because a cop tried to pull me over and I took off. When I turned onto my street, speeding beyond belief, I almost hit an oncoming car head-on. The driver swerved to get out of my way, and ended up crashing into a tree. I was fifteen and scared to death. I took off, then dumped the car. I had no idea it was my grandmother until the cops showed up at my door. This is something that has haunted me all of my life. The guilt has imprisoned me, and I pray daily for forgiveness from God. He has forgiven me, yet I can not forgive myself. So I stand before you today not to ask for your forgiveness, but to apologize and let you know that I am stepping down as pastor of Lily Grove. I don't deserve the blessings God has bestowed upon me, and I don't deserve to be your pastor. I am so sorry for the pain I have caused my family." He looked over at his aunts, who sat in shock. "And I am so sorry for the pain I have caused you. I know that I may face charges, but quite honestly, any prison time I receive can be no worse than the prison I've lived in for the past fourteen years. Church, keep me in your prayers. Keep my aunts in your prayers. And God bless you."

Terrance choked back more tears as he stepped down from the pulpit.

Almost simultaneously, Savannah, Raquel, Eva, Mamie, and Dorothy Mae jumped up and raced to the back of the church, following Terrance to his office.

By the time they all reached his office, Terrance was

removing things from his desk and putting them in a large box.

"Terrance, please tell me this is some kind of cruel joke," Eva said, tears streaming down her face. She was trembling and, for once, looked her age.

Terrance could barely look at her. "I wish it were. But, no, it's the truth." As much as it hurt, he felt a sort of peace at having the weight of what he'd done lifted from his shoulders.

"Baby, how . . . why would you . . ." Dorothy Mae couldn't even finish her sentence. She was heavily crying as well.

Terrance looked at his aunts. He was disgusted and disappointed in himself. "I don't have any answers. I ran that night because I was scared. And as each day passed, it became harder and harder for me to come clean." He picked up the five-by-seven photo of his grandmother and stared at it. "I think she knew. She saw that it was me when she swerved to get out of the way." Terrance's voice cracked. "Right before she plowed into the tree." Terrance wiped away his tears and dropped the photo in the box. "I'll never forgive myself. I've tried, but I just can't."

"But why did you think you couldn't tell us?" Eva said, stepping closer to him.

Terrance shrugged. "Scared of losing your love. Of going to jail. Ashamed of what I'd done. Devastated that I was responsible for the death of the person who loved me the most. You name it."

Savannah eased toward him as well. "Oh, Terrance. I know this is heartbreaking. Let me take you home."

Terrance cut his eyes at her. He didn't even have the

energy to be angry with her anymore. "It's over, Savannah. You don't have anything to hold over my head. You don't have anything to threaten me with, so there will be no marriage."

"She was blackmailing you?" Mamie asked as she glared at Savannah amid her own tears. "Why does that not surprise me?"

Savannah was silent. She looked like she wanted to say something, but obviously decided against it.

Terrance picked up the box. "You all will never know how sorry I am." He looked at Raquel. "Thank you for giving me the courage to face my demons. I'm so glad you're okay, but I don't deserve this church, happiness, or a woman like you." Terrance tuned out the cries of all five women as he made his way out of the church.

chapter 49

Savannah slumped against the wall in the church hallway. The tears wouldn't stop coming. Everything—her
life, her chance at redemption, her chance at happiness—
all of her dreams were gone.

Savannah buried her head in her lap just as she heard
Tyra come running down the hall, calling her name.

"Savannah! Are you okay?" Tyra squatted next to
Savannah and started stroking her hair.

"What are you doing here?" Savannah numbly asked.

"You know I promised you I was coming to church
this Sunday. But that doesn't matter. I'm worried about
you. Are you okay?"

Savannah stared at her blankly, then suddenly broke
down and began sobbing uncontrollably.

"Oh, Savannah. I'm so sorry."

"It's over, Tyra," Savannah cried as she laid her head
against Tyra's chest. "I just wanted to be happy, and it's
over."

"Shhhh," Tyra soothingly said. "It's gon' be all right.

I know it doesn't feel like it, but you'll find the man you were meant to be with."

Savannah sniffed loudly. "You don't understand, Tyra. I was so close to having people's respect. I just needed someone like Terrance in my life and people would stop putting me down so much. I'm tired of people talking about me, treating me like crap. I know I try to act like it doesn't, but it hurts and I just wanted a different life," she cried.

"Girl, cut out all that crying."

Both Savannah and Tyra looked up to see Savannah's grandmother standing over them. She had on a long-sleeve, tiger-striped rayon dress, a frayed white shawl, a fake black ponytail that hung down to her waist, and her usual overabundance of makeup.

"Ms. McKinney," Tyra began, still holding Savannah. "Savannah's a little upset right now. Now might not be the time."

Grandma Flo shot Tyra a look, like who was she to be telling her anything about her granddaughter. "I know she's upset. I was right there when her little lover told everybody he was a murderer. And wanna try and judge Savannah. Hmph!"

"What are you doing here?" Savannah sniffed. She wasn't in the mood to deal with her grandmother.

"You know I come to church every other Sunday," Grandma Flo snapped. "You just made a plumb fool out of yourself in there. Everybody standing around whispering about their murderous pastor and the tramp who was trying to make him marry her. I ain't never been so embarrassed in my life. I had to go outside and smoke me a cigarette." Flo shook her head. "I told you not to go fall in love with that boy. Love makes you do stupid things, and what you did trying to make him love you was downright stupid."

"Grandma, please. Now is not the time," Savannah sniffed.

Flo put her hands on her hips. "It sho' ain't. The time was two months ago when I told you to use him before he used you. But did you listen? Nooo. Gave that boy your time, and I'm sure your body, and what did you get out of it? Huh? What do you have to show for it? Absolutely nothing! Just pathetic." Flo walked closer, leaned down, and looked at Savannah with disgust. "I told you that boy would never want somebody like you."

"That's enough, Florence McKinney!" Dorothy Mae's voice caused all three of them to turn their heads. "Leave that girl alone."

Savannah didn't know why Dorothy Mae was coming to her defense, especially after what Savannah had done in trying to blackmail Terrance.

"Excuse me," Flo snapped as she stood up. "This is between me and my granddaughter. Don't come out here acting like you care about her."

Dorothy Mae looked like she didn't know what to say. She didn't really care about Savannah, but watching her sitting there like a wounded puppy, getting beaten down even more by her floozy of a grandmother, made Dorothy Mae feel more than a little sorry for Savannah.

"It's okay, Ms. Dorothy Mae," Savannah said, pulling herself up off the floor. She used her dress sleeve to wipe the tears from her face. "My grandmother is just being her usual self." Savannah sighed.

"You ain't got to explain nothing to this old hag

about me," Flo barked as she tossed her ponytail from side to side.

"You wanna see an old hag?" Dorothy Mae said, taking a step toward Flo.

"You feeling froggy? Jump," Flo said, removing her large gold earrings.

"Ladies, please," Raquel said, trying to diffuse the situation. She stepped in between Dorothy Mae and Flo. She looked like she couldn't believe that they were actually about to go at it. "Haven't we all been through enough?"

Flo huffed and turned back to Savannah. "And you thought these Goody Two-shoes would ever accept you into their family? Far as they concerned, you just a little ghetto chick who they thought wasn't good enough for their saved and sanctified nephew."

"If she's ghetto, she came by it honestly," Dorothy Mae retorted.

"Shouldn't you be off somewhere making sure your nephew ain't killing somebody else?" Flo growled.

Savannah stepped in because she could see Dorothy Mae was about to lose it. "Grandma, stop it!"

Flo threw her shawl over her shoulder. "Yeah, yeah, yeah. Savannah, you can stay back here and let these holier-than-thou hypocrites step on you all you want. Me, I gots me a date." She eyed Dorothy Mae. "Chester Edwards said he been looking for a real woman like me."

Eva had to squeeze Dorothy Mae's arm to get her to control the fire that was building in her eyes.

Flo giggled as she sashayed down the church hallway and out the side door.

"Everybody," Savannah said after her grandmother was out of sight, "I'm sorry about that." She lowered her head. "I'm sorry about everything." Savannah was utterly exhausted. She was tired of the games, tired of the fighting, tired of everything. And it especially hurt her heart to see the pain Terrance had put himself through today. And all because of her. Maybe if she hadn't been blackmailing him, he would've never felt the need to confess.

"I know you'll never understand why I did what I did." Savannah looked around at all five of the women. "None of you will. But trust me when I tell you, I loved Terrance."

"Do you even know what love is?" Mamie snapped, like she wasn't buying the remorseful look on Savannah's face.

Savannah sighed in defeat. "I thought I did. I thought I had found it with Terrance." She had never intended on apologizing to anyone, but she just wanted this all to be over. So what, she'd never gain their acceptance. At this point, she was just tired of trying.

"Maybe you just thought it was love because you looked at who you thought Terrance could make you into," Eva said, a sincerity across her face that Savannah had never seen before.

Savannah rubbed her forehead, which was pounding. "Maybe you're right. I just got caught up in what I wanted. I never meant to hurt anyone." She turned to Raquel. "Can you go find Terrance? Help him through this. You're the only person that can. I know that now."

Raquel stepped forward, hesitated, then reached out and hugged Savannah. "I hope you find the happiness you're searching for. I'll pray for you."

Savannah wiped at the tears that had started trickling down her cheeks again. "Thank you," she replied, as Raquel headed out the door in search of Terrance.

Eva walked over and stood in front of Savannah. Her face wasn't filled with the contempt that it usually bore, but it was still far from welcoming. "I don't condone what you did," Eva said. "But, well, we weren't perfect either."

Dorothy Mae stepped toward Savannah. "And if you have to deal with a grandmother like Florence, it's no wonder you make some messed-up decisions."

Savannah flashed a weak smile as they stood in awkward silence for a brief minute.

"Oh, so I guess we just gon' break out and sing 'We Are the World' next, huh?" Mamie snapped as she rolled her eyes. "Everybody else may be all ready to forgive and forget, but I'm not having it."

Dorothy Mae shook her head at Mamie. "As you can see, my sister is not as forgiving."

"Sho' ain't," Mamie said, folding her arms across her chest.

"It's okay," Savannah said. "You all have a lot to deal with, and I should be the least of your concerns."

"Now she's saying something I can agree with," Mamie said.

"Let it go, Mamie," Eva said. She turned back to Savannah. "It's time all of us let it go."

Eva was worn-out. She didn't want to think about Savannah anymore. She didn't want to hear her sisters bickering and complaining anymore. Right now, the only thing she could focus on was finding Terrance and convincing him that if God could forgive him, they could, too. And maybe, in turn, that would help him forgive himself.

chapter 50

Eva placed the crystal angel on top of the seven-foot-tall Christmas tree. It had been years since she'd used the doe-eyed angel. Something about her expression was so sad. Terrance had given Eva the angel the Christmas after his grandmother died. She'd thought it was an odd and depressing gift, but now she understood.

"Ms. Eva, what are you doing up on that ladder?" Raquel asked. They were all in Eva's living room, where they'd pretty much been keeping vigil for the past week. No one had heard from nor been able to get in touch with Terrance. Raquel had spent the first few days camped out on his doorstep, but he'd never come home.

"You know I got to keep busy," Eva said, stepping down off the small ladder. "Otherwise, I'm going to lose my mind."

Just as she reached the bottom, Eva had to lean against the wall to steady herself. She didn't realize she was trembling until she almost lost her balance.

"Ms. Eva, please sit down," Raquel said, trying to ease her to a chair.

"Where is he?" Eva mumbled, almost catatonic. "Why won't he let us know he's all right?" She'd tried to be strong all week, but she was at her breaking point.

Raquel wanted to cry herself. But she felt like there were no more tears left inside her.

"I'm sure it's just because he's trying to work things out himself," Raquel tried to reason.

"What if we never see him again?" Dorothy Mae said. She and Mamie had been so quiet, Raquel had almost forgotten they were in the room.

"You can't think like that," Raquel tried to comfort them. "We just have to give him some time."

"Well, I can't stay in this house going crazy," Eva said.

"It's Christmas Eve, for Christ's sake. I'm going back over there. Essie died fourteen years ago today. He doesn't need to be alone."

"But what makes you think he's going to answer the door even if he is at home?" Mamie asked.

"Then I'll just kick the door down," Eva proclaimed.

Raquel smiled as she envisioned Eva trying to kick a door in. "If it'll make you feel better, we can go by his house again and see if he's home, or if he'll even answer."

"Thank you. It would make me feel a lot better," Eva replied, already heading toward the door.

Terrance reached up and slammed the off button on his television. It seemed like every channel he'd turned to was showing something holiday-related. Even ESPN had video of football players giving away toys to underprivileged kids. He wasn't in the mood for Christmas shows, Christmas carols, Christmas reflections, or anything Christmas-related. After all, he didn't have anything to celebrate.

He'd been holed up in his house for the past week. He'd parked his car around the corner at the apartment complex so no one would know he was home and had refused to answer the door, the phone, or the text messages that everyone had been sending. He had to get his head together, figure out his next move. Part of him felt like he just needed to leave Houston, start fresh somewhere else. Maybe move to some place like Idaho. Anything to try to escape the memories and the pain that he'd caused everyone.

The sound of someone banging on his front door snapped him out of his thoughts. Of course, he'd planned to ignore it, just as he'd been doing the last few days. But his heart dropped when he heard Raquel say, "Terrance, please, I'm begging you. Open the door. I know you're in there. The note I left the other day is gone."

Terrance silently cursed. He'd started to just leave the letter there, but he'd been reading and rereading it since he found it. In it, Raquel again professed her love, and seeing that was the only reason he hadn't already left town.

"I just want you to know, I'm not leaving here," Raquel announced. "I brought a pillow and a blanket, and I'm about to set up camp right here on your doorstep until you open this door."

Terrance smiled for the first time in a week. He imagined her wrapped in a blanket at his door, a determined look across her face.

"It's supposed to be thirty degrees tonight. You wouldn't want me to die of frostbite, would you?" she called through the door.

Terrance exhaled, then made his way to the door. He swung it open and stared at Raquel. She had bags under her eyes and looked like her week had been as rough as his.

He didn't say anything as he just stepped to the side and let her pass.

"You know everybody's worried sick about you," she said, turning to him. He shut the door and turned and walked back into his living room.

"I'm sorry, I don't mean to have anyone worried about me. I just have a lot on my mind right now," Terrance solemnly said.

"And now's the time when you should be surrounded by those who love you." Raquel stared at him. She had to get through to him. He looked horrible, with hair that was screaming to be cut, and stubble that covered his entire chin.

"What part of 'I don't deserve your love' do you not get? I have to atone for my sins."

"Terrance, shake off that self-pity. It's not you," Raquel said in a tone that told him she was losing sympathy. "You made a horrible, horrible mistake. A long, long time ago. You've got to let it go. You preach all the time about forgiveness. You said yourself God has forgiven you. He's had mercy on you. So why is that not enough for you?"

Terrance stared at her. That was the million-dollar question.

Raquel continued, "Jeremiah thirty-one, thirty-four, says that when God forgives us, He remembers our sins no more. He doesn't forget, but because He forgives us, He chooses not to bring up our sin in a negative way. Forgiving yourself is simply letting go of what you are holding against yourself so that you can move on with God. If God has moved on, shouldn't we do the same?"

Terrance couldn't help but smile. "Sounds like somebody was paying attention in Bible Study."

Raquel stared back, not returning his smile. "Sounds like somebody else wasn't."

Terrance's smile faded. Raquel was revealing a painful truth. He'd preached words he wasn't heeding himself.

"Terrance, the longer you avoid forgiving yourself, the longer you allow yourself to harbor the feelings that you deserve to suffer for what you did, the more explosive you will become, and the more likely you are to hurt others. Just like you're hurting me. Just like you're hurting your aunts."

Terrance cringed at the mention of his aunts.

"Stop being a coward and face them."

Terrance raised his eyebrows at Raquel's harsh words. She folded her arms, unmoved. "I know you're dealing with a lot, but we all are. You've hurt them enough. Don't hurt them even more by shutting them out." Raquel didn't give him time to respond. "Look, you might as well know, your aunts are outside in the car. They want to come in and see you. And you need to let them."

Terrance sighed heavily before plopping down on the sofa. "I don't think I can do this," he moaned.

"You can do anything you want to do. Stop being a coward and face them. You need to deal with this," Raquel said, no longer caring if her words were too harsh. She had to snap him out of this pitiful funk he was in. "They have been worried to death. Do you know I saw Mamie cry? I didn't even think she had tear ducts."

"Aunt Mamie, crying? That must mean she was in a whole lot of pain," he tried to joke.

"Exactly. And the only thing that can bring her out of it is you. I'm going to tell them to come on in," Raquel said, looking at him for his approval.

He hesitated, then nodded. Raquel walked over to the door, opened it, and leaned outside, waving toward the car. A few minutes later, all three of his aunts stood in front of him.

An awkward silence hung in the air. Eva looked like she didn't know if she should hug him or slap him.

"Terrance Deshaun Ellis, I am so disappointed in you," Eva said. "It's not what you did, although I am devastated about that. It's the fact that you held it in for so long and tortured yourself for all these years, never feeling like you could turn to us."

"Join the club," Terrance stoically responded. "I'm disappointed in me, too."

Dorothy Mae sat down next to him. "We're not judging you because of what you did. We're not mad at you about that. I mean, we are, but we aren't. We know it was an accident."

Terrance looked at her, confused.

Eva stepped in. "I think what she's trying to say is, yes, it broke our hearts to find out you were the driver we've been searching for all these years. But we also know you. We know your heart. And we know this is worse than any prison you could've ever been in."

"But you've got to know, my sister would not want you to punish yourself like this," Dorothy Mae added.

"Yeah," Mamie echoed. "She would want you to pick yourself up, dust yourself off, and know that if God is with you, then so are we."

Terrance was quiet.

"Terrance, Lily Grove needs you. We need you." Raquel knelt in front of him, her eyes filling with tears. "*I* need you."

"Son," Eva added, sitting on the other side of him on the sofa, "the reality is that you cannot change what has happened. You can't bring your grandmother back. But you can make a difference in the lives of others. You can give back some of what you have taken away by finding a different place to invest your time and compassion. You found that at Lily Grove. So it's time to let it go."

Terrance looked at the woman who had taken over where his grandmother had left off, and fourteen years of emotion overcame him. He buried his head in Raquel's chest and cried. And for the first time, he truly felt forgiven.

chapter 51

101-Year Christmas Celebration

What a difference a year can make.

Terrance watched as the choir wrapped up a powerful rendition of "When Praises Go Up." He was thrilled at the turnout at today's service. He'd actually been apprehensive about this whole celebration because, really, who celebrates *101* years? But Raquel had convinced him that the church needed it after the disaster last year.

Raquel. The perfect pastor's wife. She'd been his voice of reason. His rock. His lifesaver. Because of her love, he'd been able to work through his demons.

He looked out in the congregation at his wife of six months. She rubbed her protruding belly. At least protruding to him. It was actually only a small mound; after all, she was only four months pregnant.

But watching her, he realized, he was the happiest man alive.

After closing out the service and bidding the guests farewell, Terrance made his way back into the sanctuary, where Raquel and his aunts were sitting around chatting.

"Hmph, did you see what that floozy Flo had on at church today?" Mamie said, shaking her head. "She looked like she belonged in a senior-citizen hoochie video."

"Aunt Mamie," Terrance admonished. "I thought we were through judging others."

"I ain't judging nobody. I'm stating a simple fact."

Raquel laughed as she took her husband's hand and pulled him down next to her. "You should know by now, you're not going to get your aunt to change."

Terrance leaned over and kissed Raquel. "I guess you're right."

"Get a room," Mamie snapped. "Good grief, trying to get your groove on in the house of the Lord."

Terrance and Raquel let out a small chuckle.

Eva smiled as she watched them together. They were the perfect couple. And to think he'd almost lost out on her. But God has a way of working everything out.

"Was that Savannah I saw at church today?" Dorothy Mae asked.

Terrance nodded. "Yep, she's doing well. She told me she's taking time to find herself."

"Hmpph, she's gon' have to do a whole lot of searching," Mamie snidely commented.

Terrance ignored her smart remark. He was extremely happy for Savannah. He'd talked to her several times over the past year. She'd apologized for everything she'd put him through and wished him and Raquel nothing but happiness. He was sure she didn't mean it at first, but eventually, she grew to accept it.

"Judge not, lest ye be judged," Terrance warned his aunt.

"Shut up, lest I shut you up," Mamie replied, wagging her finger.

Terrance grinned. "You know what I think, Aunt Mamie?"

"No, but I'm sure you'll tell me."

"I think you need a man."

Mamie rolled her eyes. "Boy, please. Ain't nothing no man can do for me."

"No, I think that's it," Terrance said.

Eva nodded. "I agree, Terrance. Why don't we get together and come up with a list of some viable candidates?"

"I have this elderly gentleman at the nursing home I volunteer at that I think would be perfect," Dorothy Mae joked. "You might have to get a bigger car to make room for his wheelchair, but I think you'll be great together."

"Or maybe Deacon Carl Baker," Eva added. "You know they're always going at it like some middle-school kids who really like each other but don't want to admit it."

"Y'all lucky I'm in the Lord's house or I'd tell you all where you could go."

"Now, Mamie, you know we're just teasing you," Eva said.

"Don't tease me. I'm too old to play games."

"Why you always got to be getting an attitude? Good Lord," Eva said, exhaling in frustration.

Terrance watched as his aunts went back and forth with their bickering. The sight actually warmed his heart. Yep, things had definitely returned to normal, and Terrance couldn't be happier.

Reader's Group Guide for
The Pastor's Wife
by ReShonda Tate Billingsley

Description

Handsome and charismatic pastor Terrance Ellis is beloved by the Lily Grove Baptist Church community. Terrance's commitment to his work leaves little time for romance and, much to the dismay of his congregation and family, he is almost thirty and still a bachelor. While the church elders and his elderly aunts vow to find Terrance a wife before the church's upcoming hundredth anniversary Christmas celebration, Terrance tentatively begins dating Savannah, a woman with a checkered past and a provocative style. As he gets to know Savannah, however, his relationship with his secretary, Raquel, begins to change in unexpected ways. One way or another, Terrance seems on his way to settling down, but the long-buried secret Savannah uncovers threatens to destroy Terrance's career and his chance at love.

Questions for Discussion

1. The church elders are extremely concerned that Terrance isn't in a relationship, going so far as to suggest hiring an actress to portray his girlfriend. Aunt Mamie says, "They think if you're thirty and single, something's wrong." Why are the elders so focused on Terrance's marital status? How is their concern different from that of his aunts?

2. Terrance's friend Monty believes that Terrance can be a father to his child without marrying the mother. Do you think Terrance's decision to marry Savannah if she is pregnant is right? Why or why not?

3. Terrance's aunt Mamie tells Savannah, "People can change. We don't believe you can." Do you agree with Mamie that some people are incapable of change? Do you think that under the right circumstances anyone can change?

4. In what ways do Terrance's shortcomings help him to be a better pastor and a better man?

5. Were Terrance's aunts right to interfere so much with his love life? Did your opinion of them change as events unfolded?

6. If you've read Billingsley's novels *Everybody Say Amen* and *Let the Church Say Amen,* you'll recognize Rachel Jackson Adams, the first lady of Zion Hill who gives a speech at Lily Grove's Christmas brunch. What parallels do you see between Savannah and Rachel? Why do you think Billingsley included Rachel in this novel?

7. What did you think about the relationship between Raquel and Dolan? Did it realistically portray the horror of domestic violence? How did you feel about the dramatic way their relationship finally ended?

8. When Terrance reveals his secret and ends his relationship with Savannah for good, Savannah says, "I just needed someone like Terrance in my life and people would stop putting me down so much. . . . I know I try to act like it doesn't, but it hurts and I just wanted a different life." Do you have any sympathy for Savannah? Did she genuinely think a relationship with Terrance would transform her? Do you believe she will truly "find herself"?

9. How does Grandmother Florence's past influence Savannah's behavior? How is it ironic that at the end of the novel, Terrance's aunts are more forgiving than Florence?

10. What did you think about Terrance after learning the secret he'd kept for fourteen years? Do you

agree that, as Eva says, "[T]his is worse than any prison [he] could've been in"? Do you believe that he has been punished enough?

11. What does this novel seem to say about the nature of both forgiveness and acceptance?

A Conversation with
ReShonda Tate Billingsley

You've given us two books about the Jackson family; any plans for a sequel to *The Pastor's Wife,* or a crossover novel featuring both families? It was fun to get a glimpse of Rachel Jackson Adams in this book.

I definitely don't have plans for a sequel, but never say never. All of my characters make appearances in my other novels. Luther and his ghetto-fabulous girlfriend Mi'chelle from *My Brother's Keeper* make an appearance in *Everybody Say Amen,* as does Mama Tee from *I Know I've Been Changed.* Rachel and Bobby even have a cameo in *My Brother's Keeper.* I love letting my characters "pay visits" to my other books.

The themes of forgiveness and overcoming one's past seem to feature prominently in your books. Have you often dealt with these concerns in your own life?

Let me clarify something to calm my mother's nerves—she didn't emotionally or physically scar me; my home life wasn't turbulent; I didn't have any serious issues of forgiveness I needed to deal with; I don't have a checkered past. But those are issues that are near to my heart because between my extended family, friends, and fifteen years in the television news business, I've seen the damage those issues can cause. That's why those are often central themes in my novels.

Do you feel that Savannah is a sympathetic character? Did you want us to sympathize with her even after her decision to blackmail Terrance?

I wanted Savannah to be complex. On one hand, I wanted the reader to see this provocative, scheming woman. But on the other, I wanted people to understand what her motivation was. It's not like she was just some mean-spirited, conniving woman. She wanted love so desperately that she went to great lengths to get it.

Terrance is a complicated character. Do you believe, as Mamie says, that mental anguish can be worse than any prison someone could be in?

Absolutely. Guilt can wear a person down, tear down their body and their spirit. I wanted to show how even a man of God was refusing to listen to the Word that tells us if God forgives our sins, why can't we? One of the difficulties people are often faced with is the inability to forgive our own sins. We pray for forgiveness and once forgiveness has been executed by God, we often resume personal punishment and torment of our own souls, which God has already said is "clean through My Son's Blood."

Like Rachel Jackson Adams from *Let the Church Say Amen* and *Everybody Say Amen,* Savannah has a checkered past but seems to want to change. Terrance

has spent his whole life doing good for others after making a fatal mistake as a teenager. Do you think everyone can change with enough work, or are some people just incapable of changing?

I think everyone is capable of change. But the desire to do so must be real and come from the heart.

Who are some of your favorite authors? How have they influenced your writing?

I am an avid reader and enjoy everyone from Mary Higgins Clark to Kimberla Lawson Roby, Eric Jerome Dickey, Victoria Christopher Murray, and Jacquelin Thomas. I also love reading books by new and upcoming authors such as Mimi Jefferson, Sherri Lewis, and Latrese Carter. The authors I enjoy influence my writing because they continue to motivate me to tell good stories.

Does your approach to writing change with every book? Do you ever find that your own writing changes the way you think about the world?

I approach each book with a simple goal—tell an entertaining story that will also enlighten and educate, while making people reflect on their own lives. Since I am an imperfect individual, there are times I still have to remind myself to practice what I preach.

You make numerous public appearances at book fairs, book club meetings, universities, and on tour.

Do you enjoy meeting your readers? Do you prefer being around an audience or the solitary time you spend creating characters and stories?

Solitary? What's that? I have three kids, a husband, and a dog. Solitary hasn't visited my house in years. I absolutely, positively love interacting with my readers. I love hearing people talk about my characters as if they were real people. I love the feedback and constructive criticism, and to hear people simply say "Your book touched my life." Next to creating the stories, meeting the readers has to be the thing I enjoy most.

Do you have a favorite of all the books you've written so far?

That's like asking me which of my kids I like best! All of my books are my favorite!

With several more books in the works and requests for appearances pouring in, you must be a master multitasker. As you become more popular with each new novel you publish, do you find it harder to balance family, career, and other commitments? How do you keep up your energy?

I would love to say I work out feverishly, drink energy drinks, and take great care of myself. But my treadmill is used to hang my clothes on, I'd much rather a glass of Kool-Aid, and my New Year's resolution to take more "me time" is still waiting to be fulfilled. But I am able to do all that I do because, one, I don't believe in idle time.

You won't catch me sitting around doing nothing. I utilize every spare moment. And second, I wouldn't be able to do a third of the things I do if it weren't for the fabulous support system of my husband, mother, sister, and cousin. I know my kids miss me when I'm on the road, but my support system helps and I think my children understand that Mommy is working to build a better life. (Plus, I need to travel now, because when they get to be teenagers, I will be at home, all up in their business, monitoring what they're doing and who they're doing it with. I'm not one of those "I respect your privacy" moms, but I digress . . .)

Activities to Enhance Your Book Club

1. Host a cozy potluck Sunday brunch or dinner (with or without Savannah's notorious hot wings). Visit www.foodnetwork.com and prepare tasty dishes featured in the novel, such as chicken Alfredo and lasagna.

2. Tyler Perry's films contain many of the same themes found in Billingsley's books, such as spiritual awakening and humorous family drama. Host a movie night and watch the blockbusters *Diary of a Mad Black Woman* and *Madea's Family Reunion*. Cast *The Pastor's Wife* and discuss who you'd like to see play the characters from the novel.

3. Learn more about the author and her upcoming tours and projects at the comprehensive website www.reshondatatebillingsley.com.

Gallery Books
proudly presents

say amen, again

ReShonda Tate Billingsley

Coming soon in summer 2011

The words echoed in Rachel's head. *I ain't one to gossip, so you ain't heard this from me . . .*

As Carmen Washington uttered those words, Rachel knew she was in for some juicy gossip. She just had no idea the gossip would involve her own husband.

Carmen acted like it pained her to share the phone call that she'd just gotten from her sister, a nurse at Hermann Hospital.

"I mean, I don't have any idea what Rev. Adams must've been thinking going into that hospital with that woman."

The blow struck Rachel like a hammer. She almost forgot that Carmen was still on the phone.

"Sister Adams, I am so sorry to be bringing you this sad, sad news. I prayed over it and the Lord said, 'Carmen, you've got to tell her.' So I did." She swallowed hard. "If there's anything I can do, you just let me know."

Rachel couldn't believe this woman. Yeah, she knew Carmen from around church, but not to the point where the woman should feel "led" to call her about something so personal.

"No, I'm okay," Rachel said. She thought about lying and saying she knew Lester had gone there, but she couldn't get the words to form. The idea was absolutely appalling.

"Is there somebody I can call for you?" Carmen asked.

Other than the list of people you're going to call and spread the gossip to as soon as you hang up the phone with me? Rachel wanted to ask. Instead she said, "No, I'll be fine. Thanks for calling."

"As soon as my sister called and told me that Rev. Adams was up in that room with that woman, I just knew I had to call my First Lady," Carmen continued.

Rachel cut her off before she could say anything else. "Okay, I appreciate that. Thank you, but I really need to go."

"Okay, First Lady. I'm going to keep you in my prayers."

"Thank you very much," Rachel replied. With trembling fingers she placed the phone back on its cradle. *I will not go into a frenzy. I will not go into a frenzy.* Rachel closed her eyes and kept repeating that to herself. But the more she said it, the more she got worked up. She felt her baby move, so she began to rub her stomach, trying to calm down herself and her baby. She let out a deep breath when her blood pressure lost some steam, then reached for the phone again. She punched in Lester's number. When he didn't answer, she found herself repeating the calming mantra over and over.

Rachel didn't realize how long her thoughts had been trapped in this tight ring when she heard someone banging on the front door. She pulled herself up off the sofa and shuffled over to the door. David was standing there looking confused.

"What's going on?" he asked, perplexed. "I've been out here for almost fifteen minutes. I saw you inside and couldn't understand why you weren't answering the door. I was just about to break the door down."

"I'm sorry," Rachel said, leaving the door open for him to follow her in. "I just have a lot on my mind."

"Where's DJ?" David asked.

Rachel had almost forgotten her nephew was there. "He's upstairs asleep in the room with Nia."

He peered closely at her. "What has you looking like you're going crazy?"

Rachel clenched her fists. "It's that tramp you called a girlfriend."

He rolled his eyes. "Look, I apologized about that. I had no idea."

"Maybe if you went to church sometime, you would have known."

"Okay," he said, holding up his hands in defense, "don't bite my head off."

Rachel relented and inhaled deeply. "I'm sorry. I'm not upset with you. I know you didn't know." She began pacing back and forth. "I'm just furious right now. This woman is at the hospital, and some kind of way she's gotten Lester to come be with her while she had her baby."

"What? Why is she in the hospital?"

"That's the million-dollar question."

"Well, he said he was . . ." David let his words trail off.

"He said what?" Rachel snapped.

David blinked nervously. "Umm, I was just saying, why did he tell you he went to the hospital?"

"I haven't talked to him."

"Maybe you should talk to him before you get worked up in a tizzy."

She shook her head tightly. "Oh, it's too late for that."

"Rach, all I'm saying is, hear the man out. You don't know what happened. You don't know why he ended up at the hospital with her. Just give him a chance to explain before you start going off."

She shot David a look like he had to know better than that. No amount of explaining could justify Lester being at the hospital with that woman as she delivered her baby.

David rolled his eyes like he knew there would be no getting through to his little sister. "You know what? Let me get my child and get out of here before the drama jumps off."

"That probably would be wise," she said. "And take Nia with you. Jordan is over a friend's. The kids need to be gone because I promise you, when Lester gets home, it's not going to be pretty."

David hurried toward the stairs to retrieve his son. "We'll all be long gone."

Rachel watched through the window as her husband paced back and forth on the front porch. She knew he was working up the nerve to come inside. Probably trying to get his lie together.

She made her way downstairs, saying yet another quick prayer for the patience to not go off the minute he set foot in the door. She poured a cup of hot tea—chamomile, for her nerves—and sat down on the sofa.

That's where she was when Lester finally decided to come inside ten minutes later.

"Umm, hi, sweetie." He was startled to see her sitting so quietly on the sofa. That alone should have told him something was wrong. "Are you okay?" he asked when she didn't respond. She'd been in a funk since the fight at church, so the calm demeanor on her face made him clutch his hands uneasily. Rachel made a decision right then that before she lost it, she would give him a chance to admit the truth.

"Hey," she replied, mustering up a smile. He leaned

over and tried to kiss her on her lips, but she deftly turned her head and let his lips meet her cheek. He stepped back and said, "How was your day?" He was studying her, no doubt trying to see if she knew anything.

"It was fine," she replied. "And yours?"

"Ummm, interesting," he stammered.

"Interesting? How so?" She flashed a fake smile again.

That seemed to make him relax some. "I just had a long day, that's all," he said, loosening his tie.

"Well, why don't you sit down and tell me all about it?"

He longingly looked toward the stairs. "Oh, well, I ah, wanted to get upstairs and see the kids before they went to sleep."

"They're not here. Nia went with David, and Jordan is still over his little friend's house."

"Oh." He hesitated. "Well, I probably should go upstairs anyway and work on my sermon for Sunday."

"No, no, come on, have a seat." She patted the sofa next to her. "I think we should talk. We haven't really talked since I left church."

Lester begrudgingly sat down.

"So what was interesting about your day?" Rachel asked as she slowly began removing his loose tie.

He looked terrified. "Well, I just had a bunch of stuff, ah, going on at church."

Rachel bit down on her bottom lip. "So, just church stuff, huh?"

Lester paused, his eyes dashing everywhere. "Umm, yeah. But I'll talk to you about it in a minute. I really have a headache, and I want to run upstairs and get some aspirin."

He jumped into action, and Rachel watched as he walked to the stairway. She could not believe he was going to lie to her.

She followed him upstairs into their bedroom. He was still fumbling with the tie. He seemed to have lost all coordination. She walked over and started slowly helping him remove it. "So, have you had a chance to talk to Mary yet?" The only conversation they'd had in the last few days was Lester telling her that he would ask Mary to leave Zion Hill and begging her to reconsider her decision to stay away.

His eyes dropped down to her hands on the tie, which she was supposed to have been loosening. "No . . . ," he slowly began.

"No?" she said, pulling the tie tighter.

He grabbed her arms to stop her. "I mean, yes. I . . . ummm, I can explain."

Rachel dropped her hands. She'd had enough. She stomped over to her walk-in closet. She reached in the back and pulled out her Louis Vuitton oversize suitcase.

"Rachel, what are you doing?"

"What does it look like, genius?" she said calmly.

"Where are you going?"

"Out. Away from your no-good, lying behind."

He stood in front of her with his mouth open.

She put her free hand on her hip. "What? You're speechless now?" She dumped the suitcase at the foot of the bed. She stomped over to the drawer and began removing some of her clothes. "So how long do you think you were going to be able to lie about going to the hospital with Mary?"

"I uh, uh . . ."

"Uh-uh, my ass." She threw a stack of clothes at him. "She had the baby? And you were there with her?"

"Rachel, no, it's not like that. Please, let me explain."

She gave him a withering look. "There is nothing you can explain about the fact that you were with her as she had her baby! Then you stand here and lie to me about it! Give me one good reason why you would even think that I would be okay with you going to the hospital with that woman?"

"I didn't intend to go to the hospital with her."

"*I didn't intend to go to the hospital with her,*" Rachel said mockingly. "You didn't intend to go to the hospital, just like you didn't intend to get her pregnant. What did you intend to do, Lester?"

"Rachel, please just hear me out."

She ignored him as she pulled open another dresser drawer and began taking her clothes out and stuffing them in the suitcase.

"I'm tired of hearing your lies. I'm tired of hearing about this humiliating position you've placed me and our family in. The fact of the matter is, I have absolutely nothing to say to you except I'm done."

"Rachel . . ." He tried to approach her.

She raised her hands to keep him off. "Lester, I'm tired." Rachel fought back the tears that were threatening to fill her eyes. "It's bad enough that I had to deal with all these hateful, hypocritical people at the church. But I fought my way through it. Then you bring this mess to my doorstep, into my home. Still, I was expected to walk around with my head held high, being a proper First Lady, wondering all along if some other woman is carrying my husband's child. I did it. I fought my way through the pain and ridicule and torment from that woman." She dropped her hands wearily. "But I have no fight left. What woman in her right mind would be able to deal with all that I've been through?"

"I know it's been difficult," he said.

"You don't know a thing," she spat. "You don't know half of what I'm feeling. You knew how I felt about Bobby, but I chose you. I made the decision to give my marriage a try. Even though Bobby was in my ear telling me that we could make it work, I made the decision to give my all to you, and this is how you repay me?"

Lester's eyes started watering up as well. "So are you wishing you had gone with Bobby?" he asked solemnly.

"Uggghhh! This isn't about Bobby!" she screamed. "You don't need to be worried about Bobby. You need to be worried about Lester and the pain you have caused me, the pain you have brought to our family. And then on top of everything else, you just plunge the knife even deeper in me by going to the hospital with her to deliver her child?"

"Rachel, baby, please hear me out," Lester pleaded.

She resumed her packing. "Lester, I'm done hearing you out. Me and the kids are leaving."

Lester's head dropped in defeat. "No, no," he finally said. "Don't disrupt the children. I'll leave."

She stopped packing and closed her suitcase.

"That's the best thing I've heard you say all day. I'll give you twenty minutes to get your stuff and get out."